HORTISHLAND

Hortishland

a novel

MARGARET LLOYD

for the evolving human spirit

HAMPTON ROADS
PUBLISHING COMPANY, INC.

Cover design by Marjoram Productions
Cover art by Frank Riccio
Cover photo by Ryan McVay, courtesy of
Digital Imagery© copyright 2001 PhotoDisc, Inc.
For information write:

Hampton Roads Publishing Company, Inc.
1125 Stoney Ridge Road
Charlottesville, VA 22902

434-296-2772
fax: 434-296-5096
e-mail: hrpc@hrpub.com
www.hrpub.com

If you are unable to order this book from your local
bookseller, you may order directly from the publisher.
Call 1-800-766-8009, toll-free.

Library of Congress Catalog Card Number: 2001092123

ISBN 1-57174-233-6

10 9 8 7 6 5 4 3 2 1

Printed on acid-free paper in Canada

HORTISHLAND

Chapter One

*I*deas are born silently and imperceptibly, yet some spring forth, as did Athena from the head of Zeus, fully armored, and ready to do battle.

For me, such was the case when the cries of this Earth, raped and pillaged and polluted for so long, and those of the creatures upon it, who were being decimated by beings who had forgotten what it is to be truly human, swelled into screams that I could no longer ignore. Added to those were the cries of humanity, itself in torment. They filled my ears, my head, and my heart. I could feel the suffering, coming from the lies, indifference, and opportunism of their industries and the governments that represented them, and from each of them to one another. Their ills, wars, cancers, homelessness, distrusts, lack of compassion or of love in any form (such pain as was never before known) they had brought upon themselves, fruits of the very same lies, indifference, injustice, and greed. The sounds howled in my ears, and the idea came to me in a flash, as if from sunlight on Athena's shield, that there must be a land somewhere that I did not know, another world where truth and love could be relearned to show us the way. It introduced itself to me as Hortishland.

Between New York State and Connecticut, about a quarter the size of Rhode Island, lies Hortishland. Hortish means spirit and truth in that language. No one that I know has ever been there, but since I live in New York, I, myself, in my little car, have tried to find it numerous times. Every time that I've thought I was there, when I pulled into a small town unknown to me, it always turned out to be either in New York or Connecticut.

My name is Phtef (pronounced Tef). That's the name my parents gave me when I was born, because thirty-seven years ago, they and their friends were fascinated by anything they could find out about Egypt. My father made up my name to demonstrate his dedication to the research they were doing, and my mother liked the sound of it so well that it became mine at a time when I had no say in the matter. While it is not an actual Egyptian name, it sounds enough like one to satisfy those who know me, and I've come to like it, though there were times when I was in school that I hated it.

Somehow I've always been different. I don't know if it's because of my name, but even as a child, I knew there were things that were important to me but that didn't seem to interest others. It feels to me as if I've been on a search most of my life, and for reasons that I don't understand, Hortishland has become more and more at the center of my search. For a while I wondered if, as my parents had made up my name, I had devised Hortishland as a figment of my imagination.

However, one day it became clear to me that I hadn't made it up. On that day, when I was working at my word processor, obeying an inner urge to write the story that had more and more obsessed me, there was a knock on my door. On opening it, I was greeted by a white-bearded old man whose sparkling eyes were both wise and humorous. He wore an unusual garment that was dark green with gold threads that flashed and glimmered as he walked. As he came into the room and looked around inquiringly, he said, "I'm Larso. I was told to find you and tell you my story."

He was taller than I had thought he was, and he held himself with great dignity as he came in. A strangely comforting glow surrounded him and filled the room, and an unexpected joy filled my heart. I felt as if I had been waiting for him for a very long time. Yet I had never doubted that he would come.

"Larso," I said, "at last you're here." I offered him a comfortable seat, brought him tea and scones, then sat down with him to hear his tale.

"I didn't want to disturb you," he said. "You've managed to find my land, magically, by listening to your heart. You've learned quite a lot about it and about the Hortish people, but there's more that you need to know. I don't have to tell you that you have been chosen to write our Hortish story. Your parents didn't know it, but your name was known to us long before they gave it to you. Your name, Phtef, means 'One Who Cares' in Hortish. You've known this intuitively most of your life, so I'm here to fill you in."

He leaned forward in his chair and looked into my eyes, and I looked into his. For a moment I was mesmerized. I could see the path of his life that had brought him here, all the painful moments and the joyful ones, stretching out to this special time, coming together now. I made my attention return to the room and got out my notebook, hoping not to miss anything he had to say.

As an Outsider, I had been wondering about many things to do with Hortishland, and it became clear that there was much that I would never have learned without Larso. He told me that there are many Hortishlands situated between states and countries all over the planet. The people know very little about the twenty-first century, and only a very few have been

able to find their way out of the invisible and nearly impene-
trable membrane that contains each Hortishland. Those few
are allowed out only for short times on important missions,
missions that are becoming ever more important as they learn
about conditions in the lands that surround them. The work is
very difficult and they must be reenergized each time they
return home. A very few remain to study and better understand the needs of Outsiders.

Larso had come on a mission to inform me and his time
was limited.

He told me that Hortishland can only be accessed by
Outsiders whose hearts are ready, and then only through
dreams or meditation. So it was no wonder that the trips I, an
Outsider, had taken to find it were unsuccessful, and that sleep
and daydreams were occupying so much of my time. The
information that Larso gave me was just what I needed, and as
I started to tell him how much he'd helped me, he said, "This
is the only time I have been given to be with you." Before I
could say another word, he vanished as if he'd never been
here, but I noticed that only a few crumbs of the scone
remained, and in the bottom of his cup I found what looked
like a tiny coin, made of a substance unknown to me. It was
stamped with the crest of Hortishland, a mountain crowned
with a star, and on the other side of the coin was a cloud.
Under the cloud were the words "Integrity" and "Love,"
which are the same words in Hortishland as in the language of
whatever land surrounds it.

I sat for a while musing after Larso left. It had been wonderful to see him looking so self-assured, as if all the doubts of
his childhood had been resolved and had jelled into confidence. I had found it strange that he could be so much older,
even while I was writing about his boyhood, but he had
assured me, "Time, in reality, does not exist." Somehow I was
able to believe him.

The way he held his head and squinted when he was looking

intently at something was just the way I remembered him as a child, and his seriousness followed by his radiant smile could only have been that of Larso, the boy I knew so well. This was so remarkable, and yet so right to me that all of those signs simply reassured me that what I had written about him was on the right track. I was glad to see, as he told me about his life, that getting older had brought out the beautiful qualities of generosity and compassion that I had learned to know were specially his.

I was well into writing the book, and what he gave me was all I needed to finish it. Here is the story I had already started before his visit, combined with the information I received from Larso, who helped me to complete it.

Chapter Two

*A*lthough not often noticed on this Earth, there are people, like Martin Luther King, Jr., and Mother Teresa, who live with one intent in mind, that of being true to the Light within them, the Light that is so easily extinguished by desires for material gain, pride, fear, and lust. They know that the Light they follow is the only Light that will lead them where they want to go, to inner Peace and Love and Joy. They may come to this understanding easily and early on, or be catapulted into it by finding satisfaction in serving others who are in need, or through their own sufferings, which teach them values that they've always yearned for, but haven't recognized before. Then their souls leap in the joy of knowing what true freedom is.

These souls are the nuclei of the communities that initiated every Hortishland. When they, these special people of Connecticut, New York, and of other parts of the globe, graduated from this earthly school, when those who loved them mourned and buried what they thought they'd lost, they did not linger there. They moved into another school, where there was work to do and more to learn. They moved to Hortishland.

There is a small town in every Hortishland. Each has a name such as Reve, Onyro, Sueno, Irrine, Traub, Son, Sapnas, Yume, Cen, or Dream, depending on what surrounds them. They are spread out in different parts of the world between many countries and each has its own special work to do.

Dream is the name of the town where this story takes place. A river called the Targyl (meaning "the vision") flows through the country and its water is clear and fresh and unpolluted. It is looked upon with great respect, and neither sewage nor trash is ever thrown into it. Many streams that come down out of the mountain chain, known as the Craggish ("the protectors"), feed into the Targyl and irrigate the rich farmland in the broad valley below.

The original settlers of Dream were Lomay and Cloa Bavres. Lomay had been transported—how he did not know—from the Outside world, as had each of the founders of all Hortish towns. Lomay's life on the Outside had been one of loving service. He had died snatching a small child from danger, racing across a street and scooping her up from the onslaught of a huge truck, and tossing her to her mother just as the truck struck him. He had arrived in Hortishland to start a new life, strong and fulfilled, and with a deep understanding of right living, as had all of his contemporaries in every Hortishland.

This was true, although they never met each other, and didn't even know that other Hortishlands existed. All found themselves, alone and on their own, chosen because of their greatness of heart, and knowing that they would guide others to find answers for those who were still on the Outside.

To Lomay, the countryside of Hortishland, which would someday become part of the town called Dream, was wonderful.

Within himself he knew the secrets of nature. He knew that without the sun there would be no life, just as there would be no life without air or water. Sun and air and water were the lifelines for every living being, though many on the Outside had forgotten that vital truth. To him each birdsong was a paean of praise. All leaves and twigs, the springing up of green, and every flower responding to the sun and air and water, was a gift to treasure. He respected this and lived and worked in harmony with the plentiful fruits of the woods and fields about him. He built a farmhouse of *tola* and *elpalm* wood, and cultivated the land around it, until he had a farm that provided all he needed. It would continue to do so for his descendants, who were to become the future residents of Dream. He named the farm Gelhanen, meaning "Serving All" in Hortish, and as soon as he had made everything ready, his life changed drastically.

One day as he stood in the field by the house he had built, he looked up into the mountains and saw six children, ranging in age from four months to seven years, coming down the side of Cranth ("Lord of the Earth," in Hortish), the tallest mountain. They were of every race and color, and with them came Cloa.

Cloa had awakened one morning to find herself in a pool of sunlight that seemed to come from a long way off. "Where am I?" she questioned the air around her. She looked at her surroundings, and saw only the rock walls of a small cave with a long entrance down which the sunlight had managed to find her. She was dressed in softly woven furry reeds that fit her body like skin. She knew that the sun would not wait for her, so she began to climb out, and as she did so she saw newts and salamanders and other curious creatures peeking out at her, scurrying off in fright when they saw her.

When she emerged from the cave, a being who called herself Philia appeared, seemingly out of nowhere. Cloa felt every cell in her body thrill when she saw Philia, who not only was beautiful but had a radiance that filled the air and enfolded Cloa in its spell.

Philia told Cloa that the Outside world she had come from was in trouble, and that she was one of the first beings chosen to bring a new culture into existence. Cloa was overcome with astonishment and fear. She had no recollection of a previous world.

Philia reassured her, "All is well, Cloa. If you will just trust your Self and the universe, you will find that everything you need will be provided for you." Then she recited to her what she called "The Laws of the Prophecy." She told Cloa that the Laws would guide her, and that she must learn them by heart and teach them wherever she could, so that they would be available whenever the need for their wisdom arose. Philia also told Cloa that if future generations lived by the Laws, Hortishland would flourish, but if they were ignored, there would be great suffering.

Philia said there was a hidden stone, the Rock of Knowing, which would have special powers, beyond even those of the Prophecy's Laws. She explained that when Hortishans were ready, when they had advanced their understanding of those Laws so that they were living them, the *Eclady* would be realized, and all would be ready. Persons of great inner beauty and strength would find the Rock of Knowing and present it to the people Outside, as a reminder of what they needed to learn if they wished to survive.

Philia had then disappeared into a glimmering mist, and Cloa, when she looked around, saw that six children were standing in a row in front of her looking expectant. She had never before seen any of them.

"Who are you?" she asked them.

"Who are you?" they replied, staring at her with wide eyes. They were all very serious. Cloa reached out and took the baby from the seven-year-old who was cheerfully carrying a being close to her own weight. "Thank you, Dagile," Cloa said. "Is that your name?"

"How did you know?" questioned the child.

"I don't know how, but somehow I know all of your

names, and I know that I am to be your mother, and am to teach and nourish you. How do you feel about that?" The rock they were standing on was covered with moss, and flowers of every color and shape bloomed all over it.

"Let's sit down and talk," said Cloa. "You, dear child, the next to oldest, are Shamos. You with the shining eyes are Tiffia. You, so shy and only three years old, are Miska; and you, little ball of curiosity, are Bian, and this precious one that I am holding is Lissa. Am I right?" All but the baby shook their heads in amazed agreement.

"I am glad that you are here," said Cloa. "This is a new world, and I will need your help many times. Now let's sing and dance, and get to know one another." The children frolicked around Cloa and she saw how lithe and innocent they were. She did not know, no more than they did, that each of them had come from sudden death in different parts of the Outside world to Hortishland, and to the same world of service that they would bring into being with Lomay.

She and the children followed a path that opened up before them, and descended into the valley where Lomay was looking up at them, shading his eyes from the setting sun. They were greeted by a very surprised man, and were as surprised by him as he was by them.

Lomay knew Cloa as soon as she came close enough to see her clearly, and she knew him deep within her being. They gazed at each other with delight. "You look just the way I knew you would," he said. "I have waited and yearned for you for a long time."

"Yes, I know," said Cloa. "I have always had you in my heart. We are soul mates."

Like Lomay, Cloa had lived a life of love and service on the Outside before arriving in Hortishland. She had died in a remote desert where food had become almost nonexistent. She had given her share, whenever she could, to the suffering mothers and babies of her tribe, in the hope that they would survive, and had felt great satisfaction in doing so even as her own life had gradually ebbed away.

Together, she and Lomay raised the children that had been allotted to them as well as five of their own. These eleven were the progenitors of all the people of Dream. Their names became family names, and their descendants took new names as it suited their fancies.

Chapter Three

The Hortish people are physically very much like Outsiders, as Hortishans call people from Connecticut, New York, and elsewhere on the Earth, but there are a few differences. They are smaller than most Outsiders. Their features are fine and delicate, but in spite of their looks they are a sturdy, energetic people. The greatest difference is that, if one looks closely, there is on every Hortish head a tiny light that shines with varying intensity depending on their well-being. It can be hidden by will and redirected to their eyes if they so choose. When it is extinguished by death the loss of that light is felt by everyone and is mourned for by all. Shared light during life gives the Hortishans insights and strengths that make their world the very special place it is. From time to time they become renewed by bringing their heads together to exchange energy.

Early generations of Hortishans were told that their forebears had originally come from the Outside, and were warned that, though they had their lights to strengthen them, they were as vulnerable as Outsiders to the same temptations and weaknesses as those they were assigned to save. Only by living the Laws of the Prophecy could they fulfill their destiny as Hortishans.

The Laws had been passed down from Cloa just as she had received them from Philia. Together, she and Lomay made it clear that it was up to each of their children to learn to live the Laws and to pass them down to future generations.

Hortishland for all of its residents is a transitory proving ground, as it will no longer exist when the residents accomplish their work. Those residents have but one chance to bring about the liberation of the embattled Outside world, to save Outsiders from annihilation, not just of the world around them, but of their inner worlds as well. That is the Hortish mission. They must get to know that their reason for being is not just an individual mission, but one for the whole community. Each must find their own special Eclady, or highest ability, to live in the love of all others and of themselves.

Chapter Four

*T*he flavor of almost anything is determined by its ingredients. In the case of chocolate ice cream, the amount and quality of the chocolate within the ice cream is the key to how delicious it is. In the case of a town, the inhabitants, their ways, their state of being, their relationships, and their communications with one another give it its flavor.

When Dream came into being, built bit by bit by succeeding descendants of Cloa and Lomay, it was a place where love and compassion reigned in harmony. Everyone knew the Power within them and knew they were there for a purpose. They were aware they must prepare for future descendants to have the tools needed to bring humanity back to knowing that all persons and things on Earth are of one cloth. They knew that a rent in that cloth would damage the whole, and that each of them would have to keep that understanding alive for every new generation. The flavor of Dream at that time was impeccable. The cloth's fabric was intact. Peace and harmony reigned.

However, with each succeeding generation, as had often occurred in the Outside world, new generations spurned their parents' beliefs and admonitions. The flavor began to lose some of its savor, and gradually turned flat. The fabric became worn. Its bright colors faded, and it was treated with less and less care, until when Gerran was born it had been torn and tossed aside and almost completely forgotten.

Now the residents of Dream had brought about a world that had little to distinguish it from Outside, the world that they had been selected to rescue.

Gerran was born in the original home of Lomay and Cloa, which had become a productive farm nestled in the arms of Cranth, the majestic mountain, just two miles east of Dream.

There, in County Raian (meaning "It Is So"), eight generations of descendants of Lomay and Cloa Bavres and their children had built their homes and made a town, while those who chose to farm had tilled the soil and poured their love and hard work into the land, growing *pallas*, *lagers*, and *brins* in their orchards and many vegetables in their gardens. The population of Dream had swollen to almost eight hundred people.

Gerran's family was the last of the line who lived in Lomay's original homestead and who cared for the earth, as had his parents, their parents, and their parents' parents.

Gerran was nineteen when the plague swooped down out of the mountains with deadly aim into nearly every home in the small county, killing all but a few of the sturdiest, then vanishing as if it had never come.

This plague was not an accident. It struck its mighty blow because like those in many other times and worlds, the people of Hortishland had lost their flavor, because the oneness that they had once known had become a tattered cloth, and because all but a few had forgotten their purpose and mission. The time had come for those who were able to learn again to be jolted back to remembrance.

Like many of their generation, Jore and Mage, Gerran's

parents, were stern, hardworking people who had served the farm as it had served them, from dawn to dark. Gerran knew his mother as always too busy to listen to him or to his siblings, although when he thought about his childhood he could remember her singing to them and trying to show her love while they did little to return it. Also at unexpected moments, he remembered times when his father's heart seemed to have peeked out at him as if from an inner prison, almost in embarrassment, especially when he had been little and had fallen or hurt himself.

Life on the farm had gradually become a far cry from what it had been for Cloa and Lomay.

Jore and Mage had each been raised by parents who had been more interested in what they gained than in what they gave. And so, with little concern for others, and having known barely anything in the way of affection themselves, they often broke the Law of love and compassion.

This was the state of most of the Hortish people before the plague. They had degenerated, until there was little to distinguish their ideas and motives from those on the Outside, and the Prophecy had become only a faint memory to a few people when the plague came down on the farm.

For Gerran and his siblings there were always endless chores to do on the farm, and if they weren't done, excuses were not accepted. His older brother, Jad, who was black, and taller than Gerran, had chafed under his parents' strict and unloving ways, and he saw little to satisfy him in farming. He had put his meager possessions in a knapsack and left home four years before. He was seventeen then, and any adventure sounded better to him than remaining on the farm. In Hortishland, genetics do not control the color or features of its inhabitants; thus there is great diversity, and unity in the diversity.

Jad's parents and many others thought he had perished in the extreme cold of the mountains at night, but a rumor persisted that he had found the hidden way out of Hortishland into the unknown dreaded world of New York City.

His older sister, Ala, had also run away, but because she had been so rebellious she was hardly missed.

Gerran, at five feet six inches, was tall for a Hortishan. He was extremely fair, with almost white hair and slanting green eyes, the third child, full of rebellion and always in competition with his older brother. He worked hard and seldom thought much about himself as he struggled to compete with Jad, who did everything well, even farming, in spite of hating everything to do with it. Gerran loved farming but was often moody because he never satisfied his own aspirations to be the best in everything he did. His parents never encouraged him or reassured him, so he had always felt inadequate and had become his own taskmaster, driving himself constantly, hoping for an occasional word of praise, which never came. There was no need for his father's willow switch to goad him on.

When the plague struck, Gerran had no time to think. He watched helplessly as pain and weakness claimed his parents, then his younger brothers and sister. He was desolate, seeing his family change from healthy people to emaciated, hideous corpses who clung to life like leaves that remain on the trees and refuse to let go before winter sets in.

Gerran did everything he could to nurse them back to health, but the disease was a wrathful, insatiable beast that devoured them, one by one, day by day.

His father, tall, gaunt, and gnarled, was the first to go quietly in his sleep. Balle and Locen, the red-cheeked, curly blond-haired twins, twelve years old, both died on the eighth day, after what seemed an eon of writhing and crying out in pain. Gerran felt useless; there seemed so little he could do for any of them, and he himself was struggling to overcome his own symptoms of the disease.

His mother, who had shrunk into a little gray-haired wisp of a woman, was nearing death, and Gerran was trying to make her comfortable, putting cold cloths on her forehead to ease her fever. He noticed her lips moving and brought his ear close to hear what she had to say. "Son, oh son," she whispered. "The Prophecy. We forgot it. It told us this would happen." Then she gave a great sigh, closed her eyes, and her light went out.

"What was she talking about?" Gerran thought. He had never heard of a prophecy, and her death was such a shock that he hardly heard her words. He pushed them back in his mind.

On the tenth day Sril, his red-headed, lively, fourteen-year-old sister, the favorite of his family, turned her head to the wall with one last groan. Her light flickered for a short time, then was quenched, leaving Gerran in the claws of terror. He did not know why he was the only one of his family who was still alive, nor did he know who else might have died or survived in Dream, whose dream had become a nightmare.

Chapter Five

No matter how strong his reluctance, Gerran realized that he must go and see the fate of his neighbors. By the latest count there had been about eight hundred residents of Dream, and the fear that what he might find could be far less held him paralyzed. For two days he dug a giant trench under the weeping cherry tree that they had all loved to watch bloom in the spring, and there he interred the remains of his family. He felt there was not enough moisture in his own body to even shed a tear.

When he could find no more to do he got into his placyl, Dream's representation of a car that had been invented by a fellow Dreamian, Golo. It was a pedaled, air-driven vehicle that held four passengers and had a bellows that propelled it faster than one could walk, while simultaneously exercising the legs of the driver. He drove reluctantly toward town as fear within him kept mounting. A wailing, moaning sob welling up in his heart went with him all the way. "What if no one is still living? What if I am the only person alive, there, or anywhere?"

Hortishland

The town seemed deserted, with not a soul in sight at a time when it was usually bustling. The door to the general store, where everyone around town usually gathered, was open. Gerran hesitated on the steps and went in.

Jom Bael, the man who owned and ran the store, was sitting on a keg of nails, his head in his hands. His light was so dim that Gerran was afraid he might be dying. He didn't even look up when Gerran entered. His clothes were dirty and wrinkled and he looked as if he hadn't slept in weeks. Gerran knew he, himself, must hardly look better, but until then, it hadn't entered his head to think of his own appearance. He was so glad to see someone else who was still alive that he wanted to dance and shout and throw things about, but Jom's state of dejection gave his heart another wrench and he stood in awe.

Jom was getting older, and sitting there he looked as if he'd added another ten years to his age and had shriveled into someone much smaller.

In the past he had been a great inspiration to most of Dream's residents. He had an inner voice that gave him reliable answers to anything he needed to know, and his customers relied on him to help them when they were unable to figure things out for themselves.

Gerran, transfixed in the doorway, made himself move. He went over and grasping Jom by his shoulders said, "Thank Heavens you're alive." Then he found himself weeping. Jom got up painfully from a deep depression, and the two embraced and clung to each other in their mutual need.

When they started to speak, words spilled out in bursts, like machine gun bullets, so that neither could hear the other. They collapsed onto two old well-worn chairs by the pot-bellied stove and stared at each other in amazement.

"When I heard your steps coming into the store I was afraid to look up," said Jom. "I was afraid I was imagining them, and it would have killed me if I had been right." Both men looked like ancient derelicts, even though Gerran was in the prime of his life. Suddenly Gerran said, "I'm starving." This was not far from the truth, as he'd forgotten to eat for several days, and Jom realized that the same was true for him.

Nine or ten days before, a few people had come into the store complaining of not feeling well, but then a deathly pall had descended over everything and Jom himself had been so ill, he had almost not made it. Living alone, he'd had only himself to care for, and had managed to drink large quantities of Dream's pure spring water. This had helped him to slowly recover.

Early that morning he had staggered into the store, not well enough to go farther, and had sat in a stupor, until Gerran walked in. He had sat there in the arms of fear, wondering what could have become of everyone else.

Nothing had left the shelves or barrels in the store for ten days. The two men were both very thirsty, and the big kettle of soup that Jom kept heated on the pot-bellied stove, summer, winter, fall, and spring (in Hortish, they're called brilt, froud, greun, and crent) was often the perfect solution to many of the residents' needs. It certainly was to his and Gerran's at that moment, and fortunately food spoils much more slowly in Hortishland than on the Outside, so the soup was still edible. The soup had become cold when the fire went out, but by lighting a few sticks of wood and adding a little water to the pot, they made it hot enough to fill their needs.

Gerran ate slowly and sparingly in silence, letting the events and emotions of those indescribable days sift through a very fine mesh, so that they would not come too fast and fell him, just as eating a large amount of food all at once would surely have done.

They felt themselves beginning to come back to life, little by little, to a life of millions of questions whose answers were fearful unknowns.

"We have to go and see who has survived," said Gerran, "but before we frighten whoever sees us by the way we look, let's get shaved and cleaned up." Neither had looked in a mirror for days, but inspecting each other now, they realized they looked more like disreputable ghosts than rescuers.

Chapter Six

*C*leaner and feeling better, they rode down the village street in the placyl. The silent presence of many specters seemed to gather around them.

The general store was the biggest and most frequented store in Dream and the information center for the town. With no one appearing there for ten days, they feared the worst for those who had usually hung around gossiping, telling stories, and keeping things lively. Sometimes Jom almost had to sweep many of them out when he closed, but now apprehension that nobody was there rode with them as they drove.

There were two other stores in the village. One was Garl's Bakery, usually hard to pass by because of the delicious scents that wafted out of the door from the buns and different breads that everyone enjoyed. The other was the Herb and Flower Shop a little farther on, and it usually had equally alluring but different scents.

Gerran had never been to either of the stores, because he and his siblings had been strictly warned, each time they made their very infrequent trips to town, not to buy anything other than what they were sent to pick up at Jom's. Now he felt a strange excitement well up within him accompanied by dread. "How well do you know the people in these stores?" he asked Jom.

"They are Dream's merchants, just as I am, and we are closer than family, since we are dependent on each other and work together to keep Dream supplied with what is needed and wanted," Jom said. "This is what I know of them. At the bakery, Tas Garl is a man whom we've all nicknamed 'Cupcake' because of his girth and good cheer and because of the wonderful bread and pies and cupcakes he sells. He has always been friendly and generous with everyone, and his jokes are legendary.

"Garl's wife Cassa, in contrast, is tall and thin and as sour as he is sweet," Jom explained. "As a girl her life was arduous, working for the people who adopted her in infancy. They had found her on their doorstep, and without any actual information decided that she was unwanted by her parents and had made a point of telling her so, unmercifully, whenever they could.

"She never knew kindness before she met Tas, and her heart, with the help of his love, has been slowly thawing. They have five children, who are very lively, and are always running about. When you're with them you have to be careful not to fall over one or another of the kids."

They walked up the path to the bakery and found the door unlocked but closed. There was no heavenly scent to greet them. They knocked, and when there was no answer, looked at each other for encouragement, then entered.

Cassa was standing close to the door, looking tall, gaunt, and desperate. She said, in a voice that came from the grave within her, "Tas is dead, and so are two of our children."

Three little figures, Milsa; Tas, Jr.; and Nila, were lying on the floor with a quilt covering them. They were still alive, but barely stirring.

Cassa turned to go back to the children. She had been keeping herself going during Tas's illness and death by tending the children, dying a little within herself when he died, and again when two of the little ones followed. As she turned away from Gerran and Jom, the rod of her will that had held her upright all that time gave way and she collapsed.

The two men were not quick enough to catch her as she fell in a heap, but they lifted her onto a comfortable chair. Jom got a damp cloth and put it on her forehead, and told her that things would be better now. They had brought a jar of soup and managed to get her to drink a little of it. Then they tenderly gave each of the three living children the remains of the soup and some of the stale bread from the store, bread that none of them had had the energy to get for themselves.

Tas's body and those of the two dead children were on the bed in the next room.

Jom said, "Cassa, we don't know how many more people we'll find have died, but we must find out and let everyone know what there is."

Cassa, on the verge of tears, thanked them. She was very glad to see them and deeply grateful. The compassion that had risen in her heart while she had nursed her husband and children throughout the plague, and with which she had responded to their helplessness and suffering, had replaced all of her previous sourness.

Gerran told Cassa that they hoped to find others who would bury Tas and the two little ones, and said they would be back as soon as possible. He asked if there was anything he and Jom could do before leaving. When Cassa said no, they took some of the remaining bread with them, and encouraging Cassa to hold on, left the bakery, and continued up the road. The next stop was the Herb and Flower Shop.

Jom said, "My friend Toin works here. He often comes to my store after work and we play a game with little stones that we invented. He works for Calile, who owns the shop and knows more about herbs than anyone else in Dream. I hope they're both all right."

The store was closed. They had to push the door open, and when they managed to enter, they found Calile, slumped on a couch, alive but very weak, close to death.

Toin had crawled to the door and had died as he tried unsuccessfully to open it. They mistook his emaciated body for a pile of rags until they realized that he had simply fallen down in the heap of cloths that he had pulled around himself in an effort to keep warm.

Jom was overcome with the horror of what he saw before him. He struggled with his feelings and did what came to him automatically. He asked Gerran to help him and together they took Toin's body into a little room that was used for drying flowers. Then they turned to Calile.

Calile's eyes had sunk into her head, and she seemed to be in a stupor, but after a little soup and some of the bread from the bakery, she managed to sit up and to speak haltingly.

"He wouldn't take any of the herbs. He was sure he would get well without them," she moaned, and tears started to trickle down her cheeks. "He knew his herbs . . . but he was . . . very . . . stubborn. They saved me . . . and would have saved him too." She put her hands over her face and sobs of grief racked her frail body.

Jom and Gerran felt so powerless that it was all they could do not to weep with her. Still, they instinctively knew that if they broke down, they would immediately be unable to give anyone else the support that they all so desperately needed.

They tenderly wrapped Toin's body in a curtain that Calile said they could use, and hoping that they would soon find helpers, promised that he would be buried as soon as possible.

Toin, like Jom, had also lived alone, and his friendship with Jom had been a very close one of comradeship, support, and encouragement for each other as much as they could.

Faced with his loss, Jom felt a gaping hole in his chest that he knew could never completely close.

Both men wondered how much more they could endure. Gerran gave Calile more soup. "You are not alone," Jom said, and then told her about the bakery. "When you feel strong enough, perhaps you can go to Cassa, and you two will be able to console each other. We are going to every house, and hope that all of those who are still alive in Dream will be motivated to help wherever they can." Jom told her they would come back as soon as they could, then he and Gerran continued on their way.

The sun was shining as they rode on. The trees and flowers were in full bloom as if trying to make up for the human tragedies all around them. Gerran and Jom drove down the road, knowing that they must check all the houses that they had the strength to go to.

"Do you know any cheerful tunes or songs?" Gerran asked. Jom started to whistle a well-known tune and Gerran joined him until Jom was seized by the realization that he was whistling a song that Toin had especially liked and had often hummed with him. He choked and couldn't go on.

Chapter Seven

$\mathcal{T}$ ime is a mystery, as is all of life. It moves on inexorably with each turn of the Earth, while every rotation makes the sun and moon appear to be rising and setting. Our hearts, too, swell and contract from beat to beat and send blood coursing through miles of arteries and veins. We know not how or why. Rivers and streams flow to the sea with gravity's help, and the sea is pulled by the moon to ebb and flow onto the skirts and edges of the land in a never ceasing, graceful dance.

However, the dance is not always graceful. Sometimes the sea is stirred into a mighty rage, a witch's cauldron of seething and lashing until it pours its wrath onto the land, destroying everything in its path.

There are moments in time that imitate those angry waves. The plague that came to Hortishland was a tsunami of the greatest force. While it wreaked its havoc, hours and days were as eternity, time stood still for many, and for some it stopped forever.

For Gerran and Jom, time now took on a terrible urgency and seemed to be surging into their lives more powerfully than the most turbulent ocean. They rushed from house to house, sometimes just in time to save a child or an exhausted adult from the claws of death scavenging the countryside.

Late in the morning they came to a field behind one of the houses where a *cladloc* was peacefully grazing, oblivious to anything other than the plentiful grass around it. A cladloc is a white beast, closely related to a unicorn, but instead of having one pointed horn, it has two, which it uses for antennae. These help the cladloc to be aware of the inner beauty or ugliness of anyone who rides on its back or wants to have it pull a placyl. The cladloc does not have to follow roads, but can rise in the air and fly anywhere within a small radius.

Gerran and Jom both had heard about such a creature, but had never before seen one. Dream is scarcely more than ten miles across at any point, and they immediately realized that they could get around much more quickly if the cladloc would take them.

They parked their placyl next to the house and walked up to the animal. Having heard that cladlocs could talk, Gerran felt shy and embarrassed, but he walked to the beautiful beast, who was not fenced in or tethered. He felt like bowing, but he put his hands behind his back, and said, "I'm Gerran and this is Jom. We need to see as many of Dream's people as possible, and as quickly as we can. Can you help us?" The cladloc lowered his head until his horns were pointing at the men, and each of them felt a powerful sensation of energy flowing through them. From the cladloc's eyes rays seemed to penetrate deep into their hearts, and they knew instantly that they would always have to be completely forthright with this extraordinary being.

"My name is Byphon and I am here to serve Priam Golo," the cladloc said, "so you must ask him, but you may also tell him that I am willing to take you."

Hortishland

Everyone called Priam Golo by his last name and most had forgotten his first. He had invented the placyl, and was the only resident of Dream who had a cladloc in his field. It had appeared there shortly after he had completed his first placyl, and he had been amazed to find it could talk (only to those whom it recognized as worthy) through its sensitive horns.

Golo was grieving for his wife, Morca, and their youngest child, Pinx, a nine-month-old girl, who, while alive, had gurgled and smiled and enchanted him. But, like so many others, both had succumbed to the plague.

Sheil, aged five, and Brul, three, Golo's two surviving children had found in Byphon a wonderful friend and teacher. Primarily, the cladloc taught them what it is to be free and at the same time to be responsible. They were always pestering him to give them a ride, but he would face them, lower his horns and check them out. "Sheil," Byphon would say, "you've not been listening to your father. Go help him in the garden as he asked you to, and give him a hug. He needs hugs just as much as you do. Then I'll give you a ride to the blue rim where all things are shining and fair. Brul, would you like to go there too?"

Brul would beam with excitement and cry out, "Yes, yes, yes, let's go now." But Byphon would shake his head and say, "Brul, have you forgotten that you left your room in a terrible mess this morning? No rides for you until it's all in order."

Gerran and Jom went to the house and knocked on the door. Jom knew Golo, but not well. When Golo had come to the store for supplies he had been pleasant but not very friendly. He was a quiet, introverted man, deep in thought much of the time, a man who had trouble making light conversation.

On that day, though, he came to the door with his two sons clinging to him. All three looked so sad and disheveled that Gerran and Jom forgot what they had planned to ask him and could only think of Golo's needs. They were glad they still had soup and bread to give the three of them and told them they would return as soon as they could.

Seeing Jom and Gerran at the door was a sign of hope for Golo, hope that he'd almost lost. They told him their needs, and Golo said that Byphon had been sent to help Hortishland so it was not up to him. They thanked him and hurried back to the cladloc.

They hitched the placyl to Byphon, and connected the empathon system, another of Golo's inventions, to his horns so that they could communicate with him. The beautiful cladloc easily lifted them above the town.

Within seconds they could see the whole of Dream below them, all of the little town and the surrounding homes, and they could come down close to any house they chose. So, with Byphon's help, they were able to save many more people than they could have without him.

By late in the day, they had visited thirty homes and had found ten people who were well and strong enough, though some were a little shaky and slow in their actions, to help them with their work and to visit other homes. One of the homes was the Prens'.

Darsa opened the front door. She was eighteen years old, lively, brown-haired, and pretty. Jom had known her from her weekly visit to his store to stock up on necessities for her mother and herself, but had had only glimpses of her, except for one time that had impressed itself on his mind as a moment of inexplicable radiance. She seemed always in a hurry and rarely stopped to chat.

Her mother, Alda, was known to the townspeople to be a difficult, demanding, and complaining woman who had taken to her bed years before when her indulgent husband, Barse, had babied her and acquiesced to her every whim, ache, and pain.

As a father, Barse was protective and loving with Darsa, and while he was living, she had been fairly free to come and go and live the normal life of a child. However, all had changed in the last two years, beginning on the day she celebrated her sixteenth birthday.

On that day he had kissed his "two girls," as he called his wife and daughter, good-bye, and had gone whistling up into the hills to gather *rengan* berries. Rengan berries are delicious to eat, but Barse made a very effective and popular cough syrup from them and bartered it through Jom's store.

He didn't come home that night and since then had not returned. Darsa's life was no longer her own. It was completely changed.

It was generally thought that Barse had gone too high up into the hills, and that the sudden bitter cold had wrapped him in its icy arms and lulled him to sleep, as it had done to others before him.

Darsa's life with her bedridden mother had become a circus of endless hoops to jump through. Never being able to please Alda, and having become the sole recipient of her constant criticisms, complaints, and demands, she saw no way to escape. She felt trapped. Resentment filled her and gnawed at her, even though she tried to smother it.

She was coming down the stairs when she heard the men knocking. She opened the door, looking wan and in shock.

Gerran recognized her from the few times he had seen her at school. One of those bratty girls like his sisters, he had thought, and she thought, looking at him, it's the farm boy who never talks to anyone. But now as he looked at Darsa, Gerran saw a young woman who had something about her that made worthless every idea he'd ever had about women. His previous dreams of girls became bubbles that floated up from him and burst in the air.

When he looked at her more clearly, he saw that Darsa was not beautiful, as the world sees beauty, but a fineness and strength enveloped her and shone from her eyes. To him her eyes were the blue of gentians in mountain meadows. He knew without a doubt that she was the one for him, in fact, the only one for him. He tried to speak but was silenced by his awe.

Fortunately, Jom, who was oblivious to what Gerran was seeing, asked, "Darsa, how is everything for you? You don't look very well."

"I've been very sick," she answered, "and my mother died, but I'm getting better. I was just about to go out to see if I could get help."

"That's why we're here," Jom said. "We've been trying to see as many Dreamians as possible to find who has survived the plague. Many have succumbed like your mother."

Gerran said, "I'm sorry your mother died."

Darsa didn't know what to say to the young man. Her face reddened, and she pointed to the cladloc. "What is that?" she asked. "What is that animal that is attached to your placyl? I've never seen anything like it before."

Byphon overheard her question and, turning his head so that his horns were pointing toward her, said, "I am a cladloc, young lady, and I live at Golo the inventor's place. I was sent to help with the work of Hortishland. Now I am needed by Jom and Gerran to speed up their trip to find out what can be done for the people of Dream because of the plague."

"I've never seen or heard of anyone like you," said Darsa, "but I'm glad you're here."

The cladloc raised his head and a brilliant rainbow surrounded them all. "You are all blessed," he said, "but we have much work to do."

Darsa's eyes widened in astonishment and her heart careened within her. She said, mostly to herself, "Something is coming into my life, something new and important!" Then she realized that the men were still there.

"My mother died several days ago," she said, "and I wasn't strong enough to go for help. It's wonderful to see you. Are there many other people in the community who are ill?" She spoke rapidly with an almost imperceptible lisp that Gerran thought was enchanting.

Darsa's lisp irritated Jom, whose hearing loss was just

enough to make him have to pay closer attention to her words. He found the effort annoying.

"You are one of the few who have survived this plague," Jom said, and then remembered that Gerran was standing beside him. "Do you know each other?" he asked.

Although Darsa had noticed Gerran as someone from her school days, she had been intent on talking with Jom, and Gerran's presence had been peripheral to her needs. Now she saw a gaunt young man with intense green slanting eyes looking at her as if he'd seen an apparition. He looked hungry and lost in a strange way.

She gave him a quizzical look. "Did I see you once in a while when I was in school?" she asked. "Do you live near here?"

Gerran found himself speaking as if in a dream. "I live on a farm about two miles from here, on the other side of town. We raise most of what we eat so we don't come to town often, but I did get to school whenever I could." Then he added, "The plague that took your mother took my whole family and many others. Jom and I are going to every house that we can today. We'll continue tomorrow until we've been to all of them, and we'll find as many well people as we can to bury the dead."

Jom asked, "Are you well enough to go to the houses of neighbors that you know and tell them that help is on the way and that we hope we'll have a meeting tomorrow afternoon if we've reached everyone by then?"

Darsa said, "I'll be glad to do anything that I can, but what about my mother? When she died I covered her and left her on her bed, but that was three days ago. I was still sick myself and didn't know what else to do."

Gerran and Jom had found several people on their trip who were well enough to get about, and had asked them to help check houses, and to do whatever was needed wherever possible.

"Two men and a woman are just behind us," said Jom, "and will bury your mother for you in any way you wish. All of them have buried members of their own families and will mourn with you as if she were their mother. Do you think that after that you may feel well enough to go to some of your neighbor's houses and save us from duplicating visits?"

"I would be very glad to," Darsa said, as she wrote a small list of the people she would visit.

Jom and Gerran thanked her as they climbed into the placyl, and Byphon took off.

Gerran didn't want to leave Darsa. Unseen colorful ribbons that he didn't understand were holding him back, yet he knew that those "ribbons" had an elasticity that would not prevent him from moving on, and he knew, just as surely, that they would not be severed.

They had visited all the households that were near the center of Dream, except for those they had assigned to others, and each time they had found survivors, no matter how many had died, they rejoiced and gave thanks with those who were left.

Now they were going farther afield to the surrounding orchards and farms, which, like Gerran's farm, supplied food and other benefits to the village. They knew that water would not be scarce, so they took with them in the placyl only what they could put together in the way of fruits and vegetables. They had given away all the soup and the bread.

They went forth into the lovely rolling countryside of Hortishland, feeling in the care of Byphon, more hopeful and encouraged than they had before.

Most of the rural families were larger than those in town, and Gerran and Jom hoped they had fared better than Gerran's family.

As they went from place to place, the needs became more apparent. Almost none of the elderly had survived, nor had infants or those who were sickly or fragile and not able to withstand the plague. So they modified what they did accordingly.

In one family of seven, Trunes, the parents, Marla and Fent, were recovering but still very ill, and two babies less than two years old had died. The three remaining children had become immobilized with fear. Brab, who was fourteen, was struggling to care for his parents and younger siblings. The death of the littlest ones had seriously depressed him, but with Jom's and Gerran's help the family was able to function again. Years later Brab became known as Dream's best baby-sitter.

Gerran often felt frustrated in dealing with children, but Jom tried to cheer him up. "Children are not always easy to handle," he said. "It takes experience, love, and a lot of patience, and none of those are your strong points. But given time they may become so. Don't worry, Gerran. Life can teach us anything if we are willing to learn." He gave Gerran a pat on his back as they left the Trune family and got into the placyl.

Byphon said good-bye to Brab and told him to come to see him at Golo's. Then they went on.

In the next house, the only one still alive was a baby boy who they thought was about five months old. They found him tucked in between his dead parents in their bed, whimpering and very hungry.

Jom said, "We certainly can't leave him here. I guess I'd better take him home with me until a relative comes to claim him."

Gerran thought, "Thank goodness Jom can take him and I don't have to."

He found a full bottle in the food keeper. The contents were still fresh and the baby guzzled it ravenously, then snuggled in Jom's arms and went to sleep. Jom felt as if his arms had become a nest, and the pain that had lined his face before finding this little one began to melt.

In the empty crib in the next room they found a finely crafted little jacket with the word "Cavin" embroidered on it. They put it on the baby, took several bottles, some diapers, and a hand-knit blanket, and went back to Byphon.

Byphon was delighted with the baby. He had a basket on

his side that they hadn't noticed before and it made a perfect bed for Cavin.

"Do you see that tree with the round balls on it?" Byphon asked. "That is a *blid* tree and those balls are filled with a liquid called *slersh*. Babies love it, and it is very good for them as well. The balls do not spoil unless they're pierced."

The men picked as many as they could take in the placyl, and Jom said, "Thank you, Byphon. You help us in so many ways. I remember now, people bringing these strange-looking balls into the store, and how they were snapped up almost before they were put on the counter." He laughed. "I never guessed I might want some myself."

Gerran said, "There are several blid trees on the farm, and I remember now that when we were small we loved to suck the fruits. They don't taste good to adults, though. I'll bring you some slersh any time you want it."

They got into their placyl and continued their search for those whom they might help. Byphon took them up into the air so they could survey Dream, their devastated town.

Wherever they went they ran into different problems. In one home no one had survived. Four people, a couple and their two children, had died in one room. Jom and Gerran wrapped each of them in sheets as they had done with so many before, and stood by them in reverence. Then they went into the rest of the house, which they found to be spotless and untouched.

Jom and Gerran were exhausted and hungry. There was plenty of food in the kitchen, as well as what they had brought with them. Nothing had rotted, though some of it had become dried out, so they were glad to have it. They took some food to Byphon, who informed them that he seldom ate, other than grazing on grass occasionally, and although he never slept, he loved the darkness of the night. He could recharge himself endlessly by looking at the stars.

They told him they were going to have something to eat and take a short nap, and he assured them they could entrust

Cavin to him. They went inside again, and settling into big comfortable chairs in the living room both fell asleep before they finished eating.

None of the animals of Dream were stricken by the plague. They had lived their lives true to their natures, and as they had nothing to learn from the sickness, they were spared. Hortish animals are different from Outside animals and only need occasional care. They are never slaughtered, but they produce many different useful products. *Cadors,* which are large bird-like animals, produce eggs that are nourishing and have no cholesterol-producing fats; *kloffs,* small, purple, eight-legged creatures, bring forth from the tops of their heads delicious patties of many colors, textures, and flavors, and these contain all the vitamins, minerals, proteins, and carbohydrates. *Drants* and several other creatures supply different kinds of foods, sweet and sour, coarse and fine, and provide the Dreamians variety and enough food for everyone to feel well fed.

The next day, they awoke early, amazed and a little embarrassed to find themselves still in the big chairs. They rejoined Byphon and Cavin, who was happily smiling and cooing at Byphon, and continued with their work. By eleven A.M., they were able to report that, with the help of the many who were willing and well enough to join them in their efforts, every house in Dream had been visited, and order was being restored in the town.

During those fateful ten days, nearly two-thirds of the population did not survive, and no one escaped some terrible loss. Only 218 people remained: just a handful of older people who were able to swim upstream against the deluge, and who could relate the history of Dream as they had known it years before; and a few small children who had had enough strength to battle the impartial bulldozer of affliction that leveled everything in its path.

All the residents had been visited and tallied in the little notebook that was the mainstay of Jom's life, not only in the plague assessment, but especially in his store, where he kept meticulous records of every transaction and inventories of everything.

Gerran and Jom were tired, but the satisfaction of having learned so much about the people of Dream and of having been able to help in so many ways was heartening.

Cavin was an extraordinary baby, gurgling and happy in Byphon's care, and the men became more and more captivated by him.

On the way back to Golo's, they talked with Byphon, who explained to them that he had been sent by the Life Guardians to serve Hortishland for the period of adjustment that would take place after the plague. The Life Guardians are an invisible group of beings who send aid to those who are under duress anywhere in the universe. Because Golo was an inventor, Byphon could make good use of his hornsights. He unhitched himself from the placyl and they got out, thanking him for his great help. He then reenergized them with his horns, and they were astounded as their weariness immediately disappeared.

Golo came out to see the two men and Cavin and asked them to have a bite to eat with him. He looked in need of someone to talk with. They went into his unkempt little house and sat down with him and his children, who seemed livelier than they had been before.

"Byphon was a great help," Jom and Gerran told Golo gratefully, "and he made the job of finding out how everyone has fared much easier. He was wonderful with this baby that we're taking with us. We're hoping someone will claim him."

In his house, Golo's two boys managed to be under their feet no matter where he put them. Gerran barked at them and unsuccessfully tried to grab them. Jom tried to quiet him and to tell him not to worry, that it was natural for children to behave like that.

Golo asked his guests to be seated, and to wait while he put his children down for a nap. The children had been going at it so hard they had become too tired to argue. When Golo returned, he said, "I hope you don't mind staying a few minutes longer. I need to talk."

Cavin had fallen asleep and Gerran and Jom were very eager to go home, but it was obvious that Golo's need was too urgent to deny. "I'm sorry," Golo said, "but I have had nobody but the children to talk with, and they are very young and demanding. Morca was a wonderful wife and mother." He wiped his eyes and shifted his heavy body in his chair. "I am desolate because she is gone, and at the same time, I'm furious with her for leaving me and at whatever has put me in this position of having to deal with all of this. I dug a grave and buried her, but that didn't help. I need time and quiet to make my inventions." He got up and paced up and down the room. "The children are good but they're too young to understand what I tell them, and their noise and constant needs drive me crazy." He stood up and, as Jom and Gerran watched, his features changed. His teeth became larger and his eyes became smaller, and a hissing sound came out of his mouth.

When Golo was six years old his mother had died, and his father had felt so bereaved that he had been unaware of his child's pain. He had not taken the time to comfort and talk to him, his only son. Golo had felt deserted and enraged that his mother left him so abruptly.

Those feelings had never gone away. They had churned about in the sealed-off part of his soul, where unresolved feelings of childhood often linger and only venture out when the wounds that have been inflamed on the first occasions are inflamed again by similar events. The loss of his much-loved wife was so reminiscent of the loss of his mother that his rage had become irrational.

Jom looked at Golo and saw the Hortish signs manifest that he had seen in other Hortishans when they began to show Outsider behavior. He realized that Golo was in jeopardy and heard a voice in his heart say, "Eclady." What's that, he thought? It sounds to me like a warning! He put his arm around Golo's shoulder. "It's been very upsetting and hard for you, we know, Golo. We hope that everyone will gather in the village this afternoon, and if you come, there will be many others with similar difficulties for you to talk with, and some may even need *your* help. Hold on, Golo. This is a very hard time for all of us."

Jom and Gerran left Golo's house, accompanied by fears and concerns for their town's distraught inventor and his children.

Chapter Eight

*A*s they rode back to the store, it was noon, and they heard the bells in the little church tower ringing to tell them that the sun had risen as high as it could on that day. The church was called Everyone's Church, because that was what it was. There was no formal religion in Dream, but from time to time, one or more people would feel the need for a place to commune with their thoughts and hearts, in peace and quiet with no distractions, or to find refuge from the things that troubled them. The little church served their purposes very well.

When Jom and Gerran heard the bells ringing, joy that the town had come back to life filled them and went with them as they sped along the rest of the way. It was four hours before everyone would meet in front of Jom's store.

Gerran had a powerful desire to go home, even though he knew he couldn't stay long. He left Jom and baby Cavin at the store, urging Jom to get a little rest. He knew it would take a while for him to refamiliarize himself with the store, which had been neglected for such a while, and to rearrange his bachelor quarters for his new little guest. Then Gerran jumped into his placyl and peddled as fast as he could to the farm.

When Jore died, Gerran had removed the reliable old fob watch from his father's trousers and put it in his own pocket. It was an unconscious gesture to keep him in touch with the past, and though he was not yet used to it, the watch gave him a new sort of pleasure to find it took just seven minutes in his placyl to get home from the town.

The white elpalm house that had been built by his ancestor Lomay and that he'd grown up in faced Gerran as he rode up to it. It didn't look different in any way, but the knowledge that no parents or brothers or sisters would ever greet him from there again hit him like a lightning bolt. He got out of the placyl and forced himself to go up the steps and into the front door.

As he walked in he heard himself using his usual salvo, and it rang in his ears. "Hi, I'm home. What's for dinner?" The silence, then the inner pain of realizing the crassness of the greeting, struck him in the pit of his stomach. He crumpled on the steps.

The old faithful farm *trog* came from out of nowhere and started licking him, wiggling, and whimpering. A trog is a Hortishland pet similar to a dog, but vegetarian and with feather-like fur. Their offspring are called *cuppies.* "It's all right, dear old Trad," Gerran said, burying his face in the trog's feathery neck. He wept. He had kept himself so busy consoling others and doing what he could for them that it was the first time he had allowed himself to recognize his own emotions. Torrents of pain, fear, and sorrow within him burst the dam he had built around his heart.

Gerran wept until the dam had crumbled and there were no more tears to shed. Trad whimpered and put his head in Gerran's lap. Cuppy and boy had grown up together, and the bond that had been forged between them helped them both. Gerran gave Trad another hug and went into the kitchen.

When life deals us our hardest blows, sometimes new

worlds open up to us and we see things that we've always been blind to before, even though they were obvious. Gerran was suddenly confronted with images of his parents and sisters and brothers, as if seeing one of those family photographs that are taken on special occasions. He could see them all looking at him as if they'd just been requested by the photographer to say "prunes" or "pickles" or something that would make them look more natural. But as he looked at them, he realized that not one of them could see him, and that during the years that he had been growing up with them, they had never really looked into each other's eyes or hearts.

A picture rose before him of his sister Sril, who was six years old when he was twelve. Her skirt had become caught on a tree branch that had broken her fall from a higher branch, but she was held there, helplessly dangling five feet above the ground. He had extricated her, and she had clung to him, a little shaken kitten, looking into his eyes for reassurance. As he remembered that moment, he felt that he was looking into the eyes of all the frightened children of the Earth, cuddling them as he was cuddling Sril. That incident had been a touchstone of compassion for him for the rest of his life.

Gerran realized that with just a little more consciousness he could have multiplied memories of such moments with every person with whom he had come in contact. It was a devastating realization, one that could never be made up for. In the past, he had lived by rote every day, doing what he did out of habit and with no thought. If his family had not all been dead, he would still have had opportunities. Now there was no way.

As he walked into the kitchen and opened the door of the food keeper, more thoughts assailed him. There is no one else to eat what's left of the food here, he thought, and no mother to scold me for eating what she planned for everyone for dinner. All of this, everything, is now mine, and I feel awful about it. "Oh, Trad," he cried aloud. "How can every thought I've ever had be changed so completely and so immediately?"

Gerran groaned and continued through the house, then went out to the orchard and to other parts of the farm. All of this was very shocking. He was only twenty and somewhat immature, but in his realization of the situation, he regressed to his childhood thinking.

He suddenly became aware that the time had passed so rapidly that he had no more time even to think before the meeting. He rushed to his placyl and drove back to town as fast as he could.

Chapter Nine

*A*ll but a very few of the people, other than those who were still not strong enough to leave their homes, gathered in front of Jom's store on that amazing day. It was a day that was later to be looked back on as the beginning of a new Dream.

They were a motley crowd of every age, some of whom had rarely been into the town before. All were survivors who had come back from hell. Some felt that they still had one foot in hell. Most of them were very curious, eager to hear what had happened to the others and what was in the wind. Children ran around, ignoring the admonitions of their parents as much as they could, dancing and chanting and tripping up the grownups. A grand sort of chaos reigned in the square.

Jom and others found several big wooden boxes and a few planks and made them into a stage, and when Gerran returned, he and Jom climbed onto it to speak. As far as the crowd was concerned, Jom and Gerran standing on their boxes might as well have been a couple of trees gracing the middle of the square. Everyone there had had so many similar trials and tribulations that the opportunity to compare their experiences was like letting air out of balloons. Some did it as slowly as they could, underplaying everything they said, while others let their stories out in one big bang, popping their balloons on the way. The noise of it all was tremendous.

So while Gerran and Jom tried several times to be heard, they were unsuccessful until Jom came out of his store with a washtub and hammer. When he started banging on the beaten-up old tub, the noise ceased, and in the silence, Jom got the attention of the crowd.

"Listen everyone," Jom yelled at the momentarily subdued crowd, "We have asked all of you to come here this afternoon to find out the needs of the community, and how we can help one another. Nearly every one of us is in deep mourning, and so we'd like to start by spending a few moments in silence to honor all of those who died from the plague and to show gratitude for all of us whose lives have been spared."

The people immediately settled down and most of them closed their eyes. Those who did not shut their eyes saw something shimmering rise from within the crowd, hover above it for a few seconds, and disappear. The children became very excited and tried to tell their parents about it, but were told to keep still and stop imagining things.

Many years later, though, when those children were older, they would still remember and talk about the momentarily beautiful sight, the evanescent colors, the glorious scent, and the light they had seen.

The effects of the plague and all that had happened and the circumstances that had to be dealt with in Dream had honed everyone's thoughts and feelings. Young children were forced to mature rapidly, and many adults learned lessons in compassion, patience, and bravery that they would never have learned without the scourge of the plague. When life resumed, so much had changed and the depletion of people and supplies was so great, they were forced to look at one another with different eyes.

Gerran tried once more to be heard, but the din had again become too loud and he was unsuccessful. Jom banged on the tub again and the noise simmered down.

"Please be quiet, just for a moment," Gerran said. "We have a lot to discuss and to settle." He had a list Jom had given him and was studying it. "Is there anyone here who knows how to stop fires and rescue people quickly?" Many hands went up, but Gerran said, "Let's wait until I've finished this list and then see who can help. Is there any one here who is a healer? Is there someone who can show us how to make the best use of our resources in ways that will benefit all of us? Can any of you teach school?"

Jom said, "The three Teant sisters, Elta, Beaca, and Gruen, and Treil Scail, who taught us and our children for so long, are gone and can't be replaced, but we'll have to have at least one teacher. Does anyone know how to keep peace and deal with conflicts that may arise, great or small? Those who think they are qualified to work on such projects, or on any others that you think of, please tell us, and let's see what we have."

He looked around at all the upturned faces surrounding him.

Drinney Fisch was the first to put a hand up. "I would like to try to teach," she said. "I love children and enjoy teaching. I've substituted from time to time for Elta when she didn't feel well, so I know a little." Drinney, looking excited, smiled at the men. "But I'll need a helper."

"We will find one for you," said Gerran and Jom together.

"How many school-age children are there?" Drinney asked.

Gerran asked Jom to give his statistics, thinking how wonderful it was that Jom kept good records. Jom pulled out his small notebook, crammed with facts, and read what he had written.

"There are only fifteen children left between the ages of six and eighteen, and only four younger than six," he read. "This is a rough count of the survivors as we went from house to house."

A gasp rose from the crowd as they heard their losses so graphically announced. The Dream schoolhouse had never been very large. It was a building that in some years before the plague had held nearly a hundred children. Then there had been four teachers and each teacher taught three grades.

Gerran had been a part-time student, his duties on the farm being considered more important than "filling your head with all that useless book stuff," as his father used to call it. But Gerran loved to read, so he would sneak books home to hide under his pillow and read until it got too dark or until he couldn't keep his eyes open any longer. Books are treasured by Hortishans. A few are made from homemade paper, but they are works of art and not used in the school. The "learning books," as they're called, have appeared in the schoolhouse mysteriously from time to time and have always been relevant to the needs of the children, and to all Hortishans.

Now the two-story building would only have the lower floor used as a school, and a single teacher with an assistant would teach everything and everyone. It was suggested that the other first-floor room be used for weaving and crafts and the upstairs rooms be kept for future needs.

Jom, who was in his sixties, looked around and asked how many people were over sixty-five. Nine women stepped forward. Jom was the only man of his age who had lived through the ordeal. Five of the nine women had had parents who knew about the Laws of the Prophecy but had given them little importance in their lives. Their mothers had recited the Laws to their daughters, and let it go at that, but even that little exposure had given each of them a foundation for their thoughts and feelings and bolstered them so that those daughters were able to learn from the difficult lives they lived before the plague. The other four women were scattered around the town, were involved with their families, and were unfamiliar with the Laws.

Gara, the oldest of the five women, had been given to a man who thought he was a victim of everything that happened to him, so he blamed Gara for it all. Mytil, another of the five, had lost a child, and each of the others had similarly suffered and transcended their pain.

Those five women were soon known as the Wise Women of Dream and were consulted by everyone who needed their help or encouragement. They became generous advisers and healers as they established themselves in the upstairs two schoolrooms.

Chapter Ten

*A*ll the Hortishans knew that there must be some explanation for the plague that had been so sudden that no one had had time to think of anything other than whether or not they would survive or of what they could do to save others. Now it was over and it needed to be evaluated.

As Gerran stood there, his mother's dying words rang in his ears: "Son, oh son. The Prophecy, we forgot it. It told us this would happen." He looked down again at the people surrounding him, and at Jom, who was so friendly and caring and helpful. From that vantage point he could see the whole square. He knew that wisdom was expected from him, but his mother's words were perplexing, and while he felt there must be something in them, the word "prophecy" and what it might mean was only a distant memory.

In the short moment that he was musing, he saw a light begin to glow on the outskirts of the square, and a woman materialize out of the air rising before the group to speak.

"I am Philia," she said. "How many of you remember the Prophecy of Illan? Does anyone know it?"

Her voice was clear and bell-like, and though it was not at all loud, everyone heard her as if she were right beside them. Some of the older Dreamians raised their hands even though their memories were vague. They knew parts of the Laws and said their parents had told them that there were seven in all and that the Prophecy was once very important, but it had been pushed back in their minds and had become considered superstitious, not worth learning. It had required something from them that they had not been willing to give, something to do with respect for and the recognition of the needs and rights of others. They realized that such ideas had been discarded, replaced by ones favoring everyone being out for himself.

Philia, tall and slim and surrounded by a rosy light, listened to the crowd. She looked ageless and had an air of mystery about her that everyone sensed. They made way for her as she came toward Gerran and Jom on their makeshift stage.

Gerran, seeing her dress shimmer as she walked, had a memory of another time when he had been small. He could not have been more than three at the time. A lovely lady had spoken to him and he had felt like the most important person in Hortishland. Her smile had filled him with delight and he had run off to his favorite hiding place to savor it before some grownup could destroy the feeling. Had it been this same woman?

Gerran helped Philia onto the box beside him, and all the townspeople stood in awe and expectancy, ready to hear what she had to say. Philia stood very still, light engulfing her. Some said later that her eyes glowed and that they could not look at her for more than a few seconds because of the strange power that flowed from her.

"I am here to tell you the story of Hortishland and of the Prophecy of Illan," Philia said. "No one is sure of where the first Hortishland was placed since there are many Hortishlands, but a Rock of Knowing was hidden in one of them in an area that has been forgotten. It must once again be discovered. It has been waiting to be found, but that will only happen when your eyes open to *see*. Now they are closed. You see only yourselves. You are asleep.

"In the beginning even before your ancestors, Lomay and Cloa, arrived, the very first person to come to one of the Hortishlands was Trera. Trera was born to accomplish just one task. She had come through the membrane as a young woman trained as a sculptor. A message had burned itself into her mind, and an urgency was in her to make it available to others. At that time she was alone, but she knew that others would arrive someday and learn from what she was about to do. Trera looked around for something to work on that would endure, and after climbing up a small heavily wooded hill, she found a rock, just visible in a clump of bushes. It was silvery rose in color and smooth, perfect for her work.

"She saw that everything she needed had been prepared for her. The Rock had a reed basket in front of it filled with things she liked to eat, and there were edible greens growing around its base. On one side of it in a knapsack were carving tools of every kind, all she could possibly use.

"Of course," she said to herself, "all has been provided." She sat quietly by the rock and gave thanks. Then she took the tools out of the knapsack and began to carve the words that had come into her mind. They were the seven Laws of the Prophecy of Illan, plus a special message that could only be translated by a being who had learned and followed the Laws and had progressed into an advanced state of awareness called Eclady—by one of those who would save the people of the Outside world. As you will remember, Illan was an ancient fiefdom, long ago forgotten except for the Laws that had successfully governed a joyous people. Their Laws were handed down from one generation to the next.

"Trera worked steadily for three days, then returned to the Outside. Once there, she had no recollection of her visit to

Hortishland or of the work she had done. However, back home she did extraordinarily beautiful work and became acclaimed for her skill and patience as a sculptor.

"Hortishland is not an accident. The All in One/One in All who is unnamable brought Hortishlands into being to attend to the dire ills of the Outside world. The allotted time to turn the tide is running out. The plague that brought so much pain to you is a direct result of ignoring and forgetting the Prophecy. You, and all Hortishans everywhere, must hunt until you find the Laws again and make them a part of your every breath.

"Outsiders have named the Unnamable "God" and have tried to make that being into their own image and likeness. They have in their pride required that this image be male, sometimes, who is to be obeyed but only to the extent that it is convenient for them. When each of you attains Eclady, you will *know* that being is great beyond your wildest dreams and that at the same time it is as intimate as your own heart."

Philia looked down at the crowd and saw their shamefaced looks. They said almost in one voice, "We really knew somewhere in the back of our minds that the Prophecy was important, but we just didn't want to pay attention and make the effort."

Philia looked at the Dreamians with compassion, "Each of you has lost many friends and family members who were very dear to you. This is a lesson that will not soon be forgotten. Now there is no more time to play. If you want to fulfill the mission that you were put here to accomplish, it is time to heed the Prophecy, or perish. You must all get to know one another well, and bring about a true community, where each is dedicated to ensuring the welfare of every other one. As such you will contribute whatever gifts you have brought with you for the good of all.

"Every month I will be with you in this square. Dream will change because you will make it change into the town you want it to be. Everybody will have a say in what takes place, and the monthly meetings will become an important part of your lives. They will require deep, intensive thinking and caring, giving hearts. They will engender wonderful times of shared ideas, humor, fun, and enjoyment, without which stagnation will once again take over. It's up to every one of you, men, women, and children. No one counts less than nor more than anyone else."

Philia smiled and raised her hand to stop them when the crowd started to clap. "My work is to help you and all Hortishans to find the progress that is needed in each of your lives so that you may all understand how to save those on the Outside from destroying themselves. Whenever that progress occurs, the Rock of Knowing will be found, wherever it is. I must leave you now, but I will see you again next month."

Philia gave Gerran a special look that made him want to carry out whatever she advised, and Jom was filled with a light that glowed from his eyes. Those in the crowd who were paying attention felt as if Philia had looked at them individually and had empowered them. Then Philia was gone, and everyone rubbed their eyes in amazement.

After she disappeared something took place in the crowd. It was as if a tornado passed through it. Everyone wanted to find the Rock of Knowing, but no one knew where to look for it. They also knew that it would not be found until they made big changes in their lives. Their world seemed to be spinning, and they were looking at each other in a new way. Those in the same family—brothers, sisters, lovers, and complete strangers—they all stared at one another as if their lives depended on seeing clearly. Gerran realized that he was seeing everything in a new light. He turned to Jom and saw that the man he had leaned on and relied on for support was not as physically strong or resilient as he had imagined.

Looking around, Gerran saw that Darsa had made her way to the stage and was looking up at him. He felt an energy new to him surge through his being. How long had she been there? She smiled at him and said, "I'd like to be Drinney's helper. Is that possible?"

Gerran caught his breath. "You startled me," he said. "Why don't you talk with Drinney and find out what she thinks she will need?"

"Thanks," Darsa said with her little lisp, then tilted her head in a way that set his heart spinning.

Gerran, who had always thought of himself as very level-headed, couldn't understand his emotions. "Wait a minute," he called after her as she was nearly out of earshot.

"What is it?" Darsa called, turning back. "Have I done something wrong?"

"No, no, no. I'm sorry to bother you," stammered Gerran. "I just wondered whether, if you were going to eat in the square with everyone this evening, you would be willing to sit with me and talk."

Darsa looked at him quizzically. "Sure, of course, I'd be glad to. There's a place under the big *cheeb* tree, a wonderful spot where I like to sit when I have time." She pointed to a magnificent copper cheeb across the square. "Will that do?"

"That would be perfect," Gerran said, and smiled shyly.

He had worked on the farm for so long, and his contact with girls had been so meager (except for his sisters and in school, where talking wasn't possible) that he didn't know how to act with a young woman. In fact, after school and on weekends Jore always had endless chores for him to do, so he'd had no time to see many people at all or to make friends. Gerran felt all arms and legs, gangly and restive, but he knew he wanted to know this girl, and was determined to take the terrifying chance of talking with her alone.

Meanwhile, others came up to ask questions and Gerran and Jom did their best to answer whatever they could or to put people in touch with those who were better informed. Before the two men got down from their perch, they took one more look at the depleted crowd below them. Many had already left the square. Jom realized he knew almost everyone by name and in his transactions with them, he had attained a good sense of who would become the leaders and who would be the most intractable.

As they stood there, a small group with an exceptionally noisy leader appeared on the edge of the crowd. They were taunting everyone and trying to stir up the children, but some of the older people drove them off.

Gerran managed to see the leader who was swearing and shaking his fist. It was Golo.

Chapter Eleven

*B*efore her father died, Darsa had had several school friends. Her closest friend was Drinney Fisch, who "swam," as her name implied, through every problem that came up with a grace and ease that Darsa envied. "How do you do it?" she would ask. "You are always so relaxed and cheerful, while I am worrying and stewing all the time."

Drinney would answer, "It's the only way I know to be, Darsa, to let go and trust. What is there to worry about other than what's been and can't be changed and what's to come that we can't ever be sure will come? Besides, we're all here for a purpose and I know of no other way to find out what it is." She'd laugh and continue working with Darsa on whatever they were doing together. One project that they especially liked was hooking rugs together, both for the satisfaction it brought them as the rug grew under their nimble fingers, as well as for the companionship it gave.

After Darsa's father's death, the web that she believed she was caught in totally enmeshed her and she seldom left the house except on seemingly endless errands for her mother. She felt as if her mother had turned into a large spider who spent her time spinning threads that were almost invisible, but which wound around her until she was virtually paralyzed. To her, her life felt completely composed of things that her mother never stopped asking for or demanding, so Darsa kept out of her sight as much as she could. But her mother called her constantly, and in their little house it was impossible to pretend she didn't hear her. She tried to pretend, but she didn't like herself for it, yet she resented the sense of entrapment.

One sunny day, before bartering at Jom's store, Darsa had seen the great cheeb tree out of the corner of her eye. The cheeb is a beautiful tree that grows only in Hortishland. Large cheebs are often sixty feet tall and fifty feet wide. Its lacy leaves are green or copper, and it provides cooling shade. The tree seemed to beckon to her and her feet took her to it, to a mossy spot where she could sit and rest against its silvery trunk. She did not know how long she sat there, but as she sat, her whole body was charged with strength and elation. She heard music like no music she'd ever heard before, and when she got up she found herself thanking the tree, knowing that something had transpired between it and herself that had brought about a special bond.

Shopping, which she had always seen as a chore, suddenly became a pleasure on that day. She smiled at Jom and surprised him so much that later he said to a friend who dropped in to chat, "I never really noticed that young woman before, but there's something about her today." His voiced trailed off as he watched Darsa go out the door, and his friend (who had been a close friend of Darsa's father) nodded in astonished agreement.

Darsa's and Gerran's picnic that evening was a shared meal of bread from Casa's newly functioning bakery and pallas Gerran had brought from the farm. Pallas are fruit, the main crop of the farm. They are yellow and have little blue spots on them. They are delicious and nutritious. Once again Darsa felt herself filled with the power of the giant cheeb, and wondered how she could be so enchanted by a tree. She took a deep breath and let the enchantment fill her with its magic. Gerran felt that magic, too.

"Do you know anyone who might help pick the pallas?" Gerran asked Darsa. "They are getting ripe fast, and there are more than I can manage alone."

"I like to pick fruit," Darsa said. "Maybe we could find some others to do it too. Perhaps Drinney might like it, and we could bring some back to Jom's store for everyone."

"Could you, Darsa? It would be a big help." Gerran did not mention bringing in others to help.

Darsa arrived at Gerran's farm the next day, and from then on they saw each other almost every day, working in the orchard or on some town project together, or sharing overlapping interests that excited them both. Gerran's shyness gradually became less as his desire to be with Darsa increased.

Darsa began to look at the tall, rangy young man in new ways. She found him strong, reticent, helpful, and concerned for her welfare. It was a new, heady feeling to have someone care about her and to be grateful for her help. It was especially gratifying to her after her years of thankless service to her mother, who had been so demanding before she died of the plague.

Each day when Darsa went back to her family's home, the lingering presence of her mother hovered over her and everything she did. She was surprised at the way she found herself, over and over again, looking for approval for what she did, as she had always done with her mother. Darsa was amazed to realize she missed her mother in spite of her crankiness and nagging, and it became clear to her that she had blamed her mother for much of her own unloving behavior, using her mother's demanding ways that annoyed her as excuses for resisting anything that she, Darsa, didn't want to do.

Spending time in the house oppressed her and squeezed her spirit until she got the garden wheelbarrow, put all of her parents' belongings in it, and made several trips into town to an abandoned shed that Jom had donated for that purpose. There she met many others on similar missions. Golo had arrived with his placyl overloaded with household items, mostly clothing and things his wife had cherished; these were things that depressed him and increased his anger whenever he saw them.

Golo's two children, Brul (with a black eye he was reluctant to talk about) and Sheil (looking thin and peaked) rode on the top of the placyl, keeping things from falling out. They were enjoying the job immensely. Helping their father had become fun, because it made them feel useful, but Golo was harsh and rough with them. Just when they were beginning to enjoy themselves, he spoiled their fun by shouting at them, bringing them back into his anger, which they didn't understand. Others who watched this felt concern for the boys.

A rumor was going around that Golo had found a group of dissatisfied, angry people to sympathize with him, and that they were to be watched out for. They had ganged up on a twelve-year-old boy and were threatening him for no apparent reason just as the boy's mother, a sturdy woman with whom few wanted to argue, turned up and chased them away.

Cassa and Calile also arrived at the shed while Golo was there. He now found himself entertained by three lively women who, each in her own way, were as lonely as he was. He had never noticed Cassa before, but that day he saw her large sorrowful eyes and observed her grace, and he took up her image to think about. Unfortunately, Golo was so self-absorbed that the pain of others never appeared to him to be relevant. His own pain filled most of his thoughts.

Chapter Twelve

*W*hen he was home, Gerran had Trad, the big family trog with his feathered ears, soft, toe-less feet, and trusting eyes, who tried to sit in his lap a lot of the time. Although the trog helped Gerran to be less lonely, the silence was hard to bear. Gerran had been used to living in a din of activity.

Working hard every day, trying to keep the farm going, and doing what he could in Dream to give Jom a hand, Gerran spent as little time in his house as he could. He would have a quick bite when he got there at the end of each day, and then fall into bed exhausted. He made every effort he could to avoid thinking about his situation. Neither he nor Darsa was doing well, living alone in empty homes.

In the past, all of Gerran's family had pitched in when the pallas were plentiful. Now there were more of them than ever, and without Darsa's help they would have fallen to the ground and rotted. It wouldn't end there, either. As soon as the pallas finished producing, lagers, Gerran's favorite fruit, would follow.

Lagers are pink and orange, a lot like a peach/plum, and have a subtle sweet/sour taste. Then there would be a lull until the brins, pale lavender and green, would become ripe, and need to be picked. Darsa could see that farming was far more demanding than she had imagined.

What soon became evident was that even when all the pallas were picked, Gerran would still need help for quite a while, and because the population of Dream was so depleted, nobody except Darsa had time to help him. Thus Darsa found herself working by his side day after day. On most days she arrived at lunchtime, but Gerran would have been working alone all morning.

Darsa usually brought bread from what had become Cassa's Bakery: She and Cassa and the three children, Milsa (seven), Tas, Jr. (five), and Nila (four) had become good friends, and Darsa often gave them a hand. The bakery, because of Philia's meetings, had changed. Everything in Dream had acquired a new meaning and a new value. Bread was appreciated as it never had been before the plague. It was looked upon as the most basic and creative food made by Hortishans, and the baking of bread was honored as a step toward the Eclady of the baker, since Eclady is often attained by honoring the sacredness of doing the work that one does with humility and desire for excellence, regardless of remuneration. Cassa and her family were a busy bunch. Milsa had become her mother's right hand in the bakery when she wasn't at school and the little ones helped, too, decorating cakes and cookies, which were much in demand. Their customers loved the originality of the baked goods, and some requested that their cookies be decorated by Nila or Tas, Jr. or Milsa.

Most of the time they were joyful as they worked, though occasionally a wistful look would appear on one of their faces, and Darsa would be reminded of how nothing could fill the places of the three (Tas, Sr., and the two other children) who were no longer with them. Cassa's tribute to Tas was that she, in her own way, had become as gracious and welcoming a proprietor as he had once been. Their bread was made with loving care and the smells of baking that wafted out the door were once more as tempting as they had ever been before the plague.

Meanwhile, one day after several weeks of working together, when Gerran and Darsa were sitting in the orchard under a tree enjoying palla nut bread, Gerran took Darsa's hand in his, upsetting the bottle of brin cider on the way. Brins are another fruit from the orchard, much like apples, but bigger and purple-green. They both tried to right it and bumped heads in the process. Gerran flushed with embarrassment and Darsa, seeing the humor of the situation, began to laugh, and then couldn't stop laughing.

Both of them stood up and Gerran, at that point feeling out of control, took Darsa in his arms and kissed her. This was the first kiss ever for either of them. It left them breathless and unable to speak, until Gerran said in a strained voice, after clearing his throat several times, "Darsa, I think we've been living alone long enough. Would you be willing to come and live with me here on the farm? Do you think we can complete each other?"

To Darsa he looked as if he wanted to run away and hide and as fast as possible. She was still having a hard time trying to stop laughing, even though she knew it was inappropriate. She held on as well as she could and said, "Gerran, when Philia was here she told me we would complete each other, and I said to her, 'What if he doesn't ask me?' 'He will,' she told me, 'You'll just have to trust that he will, and some day he'll surprise you.' You did, Gerran. She was right, and yes, I will."

In Hortishland, instead of marrying, people complete each other, which, of course, is what they're supposed to do on the Outside, and instead of a wedding there's a Giving—a giving of each to the other. They become each other's givens.

Chapter Thirteen

*H*elping Gerran was only one of the things that Darsa did from day to day. She taught school with Drinney in the mornings, and when she could, on some afternoons, she pursued her favorite occupation, which was to follow the Targyl and the little streams that branched from it, gathering reeds along the banks to make paper. She made beautiful papers from different plants, each of which gave them slightly different shades—lovely tans and taupes, and very pale greens. Some she took to Jom's store, and some she made into little books for the Dream school students. Her paper was highly valued by many Dreamians.

Several times, as she was looking for the perfect reeds, Darsa had seen paths that appeared to go up into the hills. She had been tempted to follow one or another of them, but each time, something had stopped her. Once she had started up a path, but small vines wound themselves around her feet and made it impossible for her to continue. Then, as soon as she turned back, they released her and recoiled into themselves. How amazing, Darsa had thought. The words "Rock of Knowing" flashed through her mind.

"Now I remember," she said to herself. "All Dreamians will have to have attained Eclady first before they'll be able even to hunt for the Rock." Even so, the desire to pursue the upward paths never left her.

As time passed, the papermaking was supplanted by palla picking and packing. At first Darsa had subconsciously pretended she was just doing what was needed for the community, but now the real reason could not be denied. She had fallen in love with Gerran and was about to commit herself to a new life.

Every new life has its mysteries. Where will it lead? Will the road be rocky and challenging, treacherous and painful, or will it be smooth and lift the pilgrim into realms of peace and gladness? Most paths are not clear to read in advance. They twist and turn in ways that keep us unsure of what's to come. One day a boulder may loom before us, huge and impassable, and when we despair of ever getting over or around it, it may dissolve into a mist as if to mock us. This has a way of happening when we think we are the masters of our lives and do not give the universe its due, acknowledging that it, not we, controls each breath we breathe. The universe has a way of gently, and often not so gently, reminding us to pay attention, or pay the price.

Since Jom was the only person, apart from Darsa, Gerran had to confide in, Gerran told Jom of his decision to join his life with Darsa's. Jom's advice to wait a while and learn more about the life of givens (what we call being married) almost destroyed their friendship, but Gerran respected Jom's wisdom and when he could, he tried to heed him. Still, dreams of bliss with Darsa that he had created in his head won, over the advice of anyone.

Darsa had rushed to Drinney full of hopes and excitement, and Drinney's advice had been similar to Jom's. "Wait, Darsa," she had warned. "Neither you nor Gerran are ready to give up your autonomy. Being a given is not always easy." But Darsa had stars in her eyes that prevented her from seeing beyond herself, and the lovelorn young couple continued with their plans.

"Why do you think our friends want us to wait?" Darsa asked Gerran one day when they were fruit-picking.

"It doesn't matter," Gerran answered. "We are happy when we are together, aren't we? And you fulfill my needs. My house is more than large enough for both of us, and we both feel lonely, you alone in your house and I in mine. I suppose we could wait, but I like everything to be in order, and if we are givens you can move here to the farm with me, and know that it is your home, too."

Darsa went over to the bench that was under the brin tree. Gerran went with her and sat beside her. "I love you," Darsa said, taking his hand in both of hers. "I want our giving to last and last, and not fall apart as so many of our friends' have. I'm afraid and I don't know why. Please hold me close to you. Philia says we have work to do. Do you think we can make it?"

Gerran put his arms around her and said, "That's not what I'm concerned about, my love. I'm sure it will all come about just fine. There is everything here that we want or need, and we will be busy enough just working from day to day."

Gerran tipped Darsa's head back and kissed her. Then, picking the most beautiful palla he could find, he put it in her hands.

"There," he said. "We'll have a good life together. I have no doubts. You are the woman for me, and I am right for you. We don't need to worry."

A twinge of fear ran through Darsa and her eyes filled with tears as she looked at Gerran, wanting so much to give him her complete trust. It's amazing, she thought. He is so strong and I love to look at him, and yet I feel as if he is half blind, seeing only what he wants to see, that he is not conscious of or interested in the thoughts and feelings of others.

During the ensuing days the young couple's lives became a lively dance as they worked to convert their separate living quarters into one. Telling others of their decision and getting used to the idea that they had committed to joining their lives kept the dance animated. They both had moments of terror when they wondered how they had ever thought of such a thing, but the excitement of their hopes for the future canceled out their fears.

Gerran was so busy harvesting fruits and vegetables and taking them in to Jom's store that sometimes he was hardly aware of anything changing at all. His house and the land around it were not very different from what he had always known, though without his family there was a heavy pall over everything.

For Darsa, it was a whole new world. She had to take her possessions from her family's house and find places for them in Gerran's, and sometimes he couldn't see why she felt she had to move his own family's things around. He'd never heard that women have nesting urges that cannot be denied. Gradually the idea of being together and of having a shared life won over their indecision and fears.

Darsa asked Drinney, Cassa, and Calile to be with her at the giving, and Gerran asked Jom and Golo to stand with him, although he had hardly seen Golo since he'd returned Byphon to his field.

After that Golo had secluded himself in his home and only a few of his dissident friends were allowed to join him to express their anger and dissatisfaction with everything.

He did not accept Gerran's invitation, but Jom was pleased to. Gerran knew that Jom was still the best friend he could have, and Jom had not been upset by Gerran's decision to ignore his advice, to not go ahead with the giving. Everyone must think for himself and learn from the consequences, Jom thought.

The closeness between Drinney and Darsa was unshatterable,

and Drinney did all she could to help Darsa get ready for the celebration.

The town was ready for a joyful event and on a sparkling evening in greun, the season of harvests, they all met in Everyone's Church. The church was filled with flowers, long-stemmed *tillias,* with their opalescent petals and glorious fragrance, blue and purple *pardias* with velvety faces, and pure white sparkling *cridles,* delicate and petite, setting off the other flowers.

Some of the village people who felt they knew Gerran, from the meeting in the square and from chatting with him and Darsa at the picnic, found their invitations at Jom's store. Jom had given them to anyone who stopped by to trade. All worked together with care and love to decorate the church for the occasion, and with Philia's help, they were becoming a well-knit community. Only about fifty people could fit into the little church, but the rest of the Dreamians good-naturedly stood outside, yet by some mystery, they felt just as much included in the celebration as those within.

There were moments when Darsa and Gerran felt sad that neither had family members to be with them. Theirs was the first giving since the plague, and they were aware that they were setting a precedent. They decided they would each speak of their commitment to the other and not about the paths that had brought them there. The past was another time. It had died in the plague and had to be left behind so that what was to come could thrust up new shoots that would grow and produce fruit.

Philia was already there when they arrived at the church. She was beautiful and radiant as always, and they knew she was there to support them in every way.

Darsa wore a plain, pale blue dress the color of the sky. It was made of a fine and soft fabric that she had woven on her loom several years before, secretly suspecting it would become her giving dress. It was full length with long sleeves and simple lines. Gerran had found the suit (with pantaloons and tunic) that his father had worn when he had joined his given twenty-five years earlier. The cloth, woven by Gerran's grandmother, was a very light violet, which she imagined to be the color of spirit.

Philia greeted them as they entered the church. "Darsa and Gerran," she said. "Welcome to this special day in your lives."

It was evening, and Philia led them up the aisle to the small dais, where the three turned and faced the assembled guests. Philia spoke in a voice that was music to every ear, a sound like flowing water and whispering leaves. She was clothed in the palest opaque pink light, yet no fabric was discernible.

"This day represents a beginning far greater than any of you suspect," Philia announced. "With it, the time of *Dalagah* has arrived, and all Hortishlands will be changed. Remember this in future years and thank the One for bringing it about. The Dalagah, the first steps toward Eclady, begins now, here, with the completing. Darsa and Gerran are prototypes of those from whom you have all evolved. This union will help the Eclady to come about for all and help bring everyone into the new, special understanding of life and love. The Rock of Knowing will then be found, and its secrets revealed."

Chapter Fourteen

The trip from darkness to light, from ignorance to understanding, may only take an instant, but the climb up to such insights is often long, perilous, and painful. The stars on that clear night of the giving ceremony emerged one by one until the sky appeared to be lit with their glory. They twinkled high above and looked down upon the gathering that was celebrating. It was a night of great beauty.

Darsa stood before her fellow Dreamians seeing herself and them in an entirely new light. She understood that each was enacting an ageless rite, and that every part of this rite connected them to one another. The scent of flowers made her giddy. Suddenly she found her lips moving, and words of great clarity she barely knew came out of her mouth, loud enough for all to hear.

As Darsa spoke, Drinney said to Cassa, "I knew there was something very special about Darsa from the beginning, but this is more than I even imagined."

Gerran was suddenly terrified. Who is this woman? he thought. She has become so close to me that we have committed to spending our lives together, but here is someone that I have yet to know. He wanted to get away, but his legs were rooted to the ground and he couldn't take a step. He began to listen more carefully.

"That's what I hear," Darsa was saying. "Someone is telling me that the new era will bring a different way of seeing for Dream, and that it will depend more on the fruits of this giving than on the happiness of it. My relationship to Gerran and his to me will mirror the Outside world. As we learn, so will you, too." Darsa looked bewildered, and turned to Gerran, who was more stunned than she, and then to Philia.

"It's all right, Darsa," Philia said, putting her arm around the frightened young woman. "You heard the voice of the One in All who brought all Hortishlands into being. Though not visible, the One is always with us, as well as during this celebration that starts you on the new path. If your hearts are open, you will learn much that will help you get to your destination. When and how that will be is for each of you to ascertain and to bring about."

As Philia spoke, Gerran felt himself standing taller than he ever remembered being, and his lips began to move with no volition on his part and he spoke:

"I, Gerran, will learn and grow with Darsa. We will have children, and they will bring about what is needed to help us realign those on the Outside. We must understand that the fate of the Outside is also our fate. We must always keep that in mind. We are here today, not only to commit to one another, but to let the community know that the work must be shared by everyone." His words came slowly but clearly, then he gradually regained his senses.

Philia smiled, and her eyes filled with a tenderness that blessed the two beside her. What they felt seemed like the hug of soft, strong wings. They looked at each other in astonishment.

"Now it's time for each of you to say what you came here to say," said Philia. "Gerran, do commence."

Gerran felt his heart pounding. He had practiced his speech many times in anticipation of this moment, but suddenly it seemed strange and unreal. He looked at Darsa. She looked so young and vulnerable that he forgot his fears and wanted to vanquish the world for her.

"Darsa," he said, "today we publicly proclaim our desire to start a new life together as is the custom in all Hortishlands. There are no living members left in either of our families. This means that we will make decisions that will have to come from our own knowledge and experience. We no longer have parents to carry our burdens for us. We will have to be examples for others as we carry our own burdens. Nearly everyone here has known similar losses. This makes them our family and us theirs, so here we are becoming one with many. From now on I hope to be for you the support and caring that all people yearn for. I'd like to give you beautiful flowers, dance with you to the moon, put my heart at your feet, and present you with the best fruits and vegetables of my garden. I see you as my equal, and your freedom as my freedom. I believe that in trust and love the strongest bonds are forged, and I hope that our bond will be as strong as wisteria vines and as free as the wind."

Gerran had learned most of his speech from the early completing rituals that had been passed down for generations. He thought the words sounded fine and impressive, and though he hadn't considered them very deeply, he hoped he could carry them out. Even so, they were not very real to him. He was pleased that he'd added the fruits and vegetables bit as his own contribution.

As Darsa heard Gerran's words, she thought: No more alone, no more the dutiful daughter, no more under a demanding mother. It's all so new, but I'm afraid to hope.

She stood there looking frail and delicate, but knowing in

her heart that she was strong, a fine steel wire that could bind things together in times of stress.

"Gerran," Darsa replied in her own words, "we hardly know each other, but we have been brought together by an unknown force with unmistakable energy and purpose. I believe this is meant to be. I love your strength, and the way your eyes light up when you envision the future. I feel a power greater than either of us drawing us together, and I am eager to go with it wherever it may take us. I put my hand in yours. Let us go forward together." She looked into his eyes, and saw his heart, vulnerable, proud, and at times, cold, unsure yet passionate, depending on his mood. He saw her heart, yearning to give love and to receive it and resentful when not recognized for work well done. Their kiss became a prayer.

They joined hands and turned to face their friends, old and new, with whom they would bring into being a new and different Dream, one that, with the concerted efforts of all, would change the world for better or worse.

Philia spoke once more. "In the future, in the time of the Eclady that is just beginning, there will be no time to waste. Each and every Hortishan will have to come to their own Eclady to be ready to help Outsiders. Now it is important to make the most of every bit of time available. Those of you who have lived through the plague need to turn a splintered world into a healthy community.

"There are only eleven people left old enough to be called elders. Most of their contemporaries were not strong enough to withstand the plague. Only one is a man—Jom. Until now many of you Dreamians have lived superficial lives and mostly by rote, giving little thought to *why* you are here. A few of you have lived fully and have delved deeply into life's meaning. Your light is needed to show the way to the others.

"Five of these eleven have been chosen to serve as contemplative elders. They will be always available to be consulted by those who want to know more about the past or who want to learn from them. They will be called the Wise Women and will share whatever wisdom they've gleaned in their long lives. But the new Dream must not be modeled on the era that has just passed. If you can't do better than that, another plague will come and Hortishlands will fail in their mission."

Philia smiled and raised her hands in blessing, and from each of her fingers multicolored lights streamed forth, bathing the young couple and everyone else. All felt new strength flow through them, and the fear that had begun to grip their hearts dissipated, leaving only the reminder that there was much that still needed to be done.

The ceremony being complete, Darsa and Gerran approached the entrance of the church, Drinney, Jom, Calile, and Cassa preceding them. The four attendants formed a row that was added to by everyone else, until there was a friendly wall stretching before the couple on both sides of their path, and Philia walked slowly before them.

Chapter Fifteen

*A*s the young couple came out of the church after the ceremony, the wall of Dreamians moved toward them. The couple greeted them all, one by one, in a special Dreamian manner. The most usual way in Dream was to exchange energy by bringing heads together, then with a hand on the other's shoulder to look deeply and silently into the other's eyes. Some who were shy and had not ventured out much in the past merely smiled and bowed, while others put a hand up to meet the hands of Gerran or Darsa.

It was a wonderful opportunity for the newly joined to meet, and to feel the diversity and goodwill of their neighbors with whom they expected to be interacting from then on. Even though Dream's population had shrunk so much, they realized that there were still many who would have to get to know one another much better, and that they would have to learn with them if a true community was to be created.

Many of the guests had brought homemade dishes based

on produce from their gardens, while others had concocted delicious drinks made from the fruits of their orchards. It was a gala time, yet still it was a serious time as the residents of Dream gave thanks for their survival and for the first giving in their community since the plague.

Philia walked on along the human wall, and her face radiated satisfaction. It was clear to her that these Hortish souls were sturdy, as demonstrated by their emergence from the plague and through their enthusiasm for living. She felt hope for the accomplishment of their mission. She greeted each in such a way that every one felt as if he or she were a special Hortishan. Philia turned to the crowd and said, "We will all meet again next week in the square for our first monthly meeting." Then she was gone.

Unique and beautiful music immediately broke out from many handmade, homemade instruments. The players had learned to make wonderful sounds by trial and error, having carved their own pipes and horns and gongs and drums.

Gerran and Darsa felt as if they were in a dream, and when they thought no one would notice, slipped away from the joyous party, which seemed to have no intention of ending soon. They walked hand in hand down the road to the home that Gerran had known all his life, the one that would now be Darsa's as well. The beautiful, well-built old farmhouse that Lomay had made generations earlier seemed to reach out and offer them a haven in which to begin their lives together.

The late-rising moon, with all its light and mystery, shone down through the leaves of the *plamset* trees bordering the road and, as they walked along, the newly givens began to feel the immensity of their commitment. Darsa stopped in a pool of light and grasped Gerran's hands. "I'm scared," she said. "I don't know why, except that I feel as if we've taken on something that is bigger than we are. I'm afraid." Her voice trailed off, and Gerran took her in his arms.

"I'm afraid too," he said. "I don't even understand the

words that came out of my mouth. They sounded wonderful, but were way beyond me."

"Oh, Gerran," Darsa gasped. "Hold me close. I don't feel as if I know you very well, and neither of us knows what's coming. I've often heard that the worst fear is that of the unknown, and maybe that's true." She found herself crying.

Gerran was astonished. Women and their emotions had always been beyond his understanding. His mother had been stern and rarely ever laughed, and he thought his sisters silly. Now Darsa, who had seemed such a bulwark, was crying. He felt annoyance rising in him, but he put his arm around her and they continued down the road. The best he could do was to say, "Don't forget, Philia said she would help us."

Darsa felt the longings that had drawn her and Gerran together return and, holding his hand tightly in hers, she said, "We'll make it, my love. I know we will."

Gerran's misgivings subsided with hers as they approached the simple old white farmhouse. Faithful Trad, who had been having fitful dreams on the front verandah, awoke to the sound of their voices and rushed out to greet them.

The Hortish owl, high in the elpalm tree by the house spoke to them. "Listen, listen, and learn wisdom," it said.

"We will, with the help of the community," Darsa heard herself saying in response.

Gerran—he had heard it was the right thing to do—lifted Darsa in his arms and carried her into the house.

Chapter Sixteen

*J*n the Outside world, most often when young men and women decide to commit to each other they are not just young in body, but are also children of inexperience who have lived in the protective care of their parents and their community. They have been given little autonomy and have not contemplated in any depth what they want to gain from or give to life. The realization that they suddenly have the freedom to make, or not make, decisions that could produce Earth-shaking results for them and their partners can be terrifying. For many, the best response may seem to be to stay within the boundaries they have been trained not to pass beyond. Thus they spend the rest of their lives in the relative safety of boredom and restraint, never experiencing the joy of knowing their spirits have the power to fly.

Their psychological age may be preadolescent, and they may not progress much further beyond this, unless life, as it so often does in its wisdom, presents them with decisions to make that, to survive, they must address in a mature way. Still, if some drastic event leaves them standing naked on the shore of despair, they may remain there, seeing themselves as tragic victims. However, if they have the courage and the depth to look further they will make the choice that leads to sanity.

Gerran and Darsa were in their own ways situated in these same dilemmas of immaturity. Having had their giving take place at the height of the harvesting season, there was very little time for the pair to consider anything other than the work of the farm. Darsa and Gerran's lives were filled from dawn to dusk, from "can't see to can't see," as farmers sometimes say.

They were busy with all the needs of the farm. Gerran was in the garden and orchards, doing all the heaviest work, while Darsa was in the garden and kitchen, cooking and preserving all the wonderful fruits and vegetables that the fertile, well-cared-for Hortish soil produced.

They were hardly aware of how fast time was passing, as life held them in a silken cocoon of busyness that required little thought. When evening came there were constant surprises for each of them as they began to know each other better. Darsa's lisp and the way she tilted her head always fascinated Gerran. He would laugh and lift her up and tell her how lovely she was, and Darsa would tease him, telling him she was going to give him all the things he didn't like to eat. Then she'd bring in his favorite foods, cooked the way he liked them best. They'd hug and laugh and say how fortunate they were to have found each other.

Everything they needed was in their day-to-day lives, and they were so busy that they forgot the welfare of the community, and it got pushed into a far-off corner of their minds.

Six months passed in this idyllic way. They missed the monthly meetings with Philia and only went to town to deliver their produce to Jom. He encouraged them to attend, but as soon as they returned to the farm, they would forget or make excuses. Darsa began to realize that she must be new lifing, as being pregnant is called in Hortishland. She said nothing to

Gerran, thinking it might prove not to be true, but one day, morning sickness caught up with her at breakfast. Even the smell of food was too much for her, and she ran out of the room. Gerran rushed after her in alarm.

"What's the matter, Darsa," he asked, fear mounting in his voice. "Are you ill? What have you been eating?"

Darsa put her hand on his arm, "It's all right, Gerran," she reassured him. "I'll tell you all about it tonight. I have a surprise for you. Please, go on out to the orchard. You have so much work to do, and it won't wait."

Recently, the fruit on the trees had been falling off before it was ripe. Gerran was worried about it and was trying to save what he could. Still, he went out the door reluctantly, telling Darsa to call him if she needed him, and Darsa kissed him good-bye, trying to look as healthy as she could.

When Gerran came home that evening, he found a glass of his favorite palla wine and a plate of lager tarts on a small table next to his big comfortable chair. He had worked frantically all day and was afraid that he was losing his whole crop.

Ever since the plague, panic had seized him whenever he heard or thought of there being even a hint of sickness in anyone or anything. This day had been a discouraging one in the ailing orchard, and he had returned home feeling very tired. He collapsed gratefully into his chair.

"Is this the surprise you promised me?" he asked wanly as he took a sip of the wine.

"Not quite," said Darsa, settling onto his lap and putting her head on his shoulder.

Why do I feel as if something terrible is about to happen? Gerran thought to himself. He felt a twinge of apprehension ripple over him. He took Darsa's face in his hands and looked into her eyes. "I've been worrying about you all day," he said. "Are you sick?"

Darsa snuggled deeper into his lap like a wild thing trying to take cover.

"Gerran, *golban*" (meaning "the one I love" in Hortish), she whispered in his ear. "I'm not sick. I hope this will make you happy. I'm new lifing. We're going to have a baby."

Gerran stiffened slightly, and in that moment transmitted his consternation to Darsa. Fear wound itself around him, like a constricting snake, and paralysis set in. He didn't know what to say. Although he'd spoken about children at the given, it had not been a reality for him. Somehow he had put the idea of children in the back of his mind, along with all the negative things he didn't want to think about, and now he wasn't ready for what he was hearing.

Problems with his crops added to his apprehension. The pallas were falling off the trees more and more, no matter what he did. He felt the ground slipping away beneath him. Even the secure life that they had begun to establish together was changing, as if the landslide he sensed was turning into an avalanche, taking him with it.

He felt Darsa shift a little, and he came back to reality. "Golban, Darsa," he said with as much enthusiasm as he could muster. "I know you will be a wonderful mother."

That was not what Darsa had hoped to hear. "He's not glad. He doesn't want a child. He doesn't really love me," she thought. The message she received when he had stiffened had been a blow, and Darsa had felt a chill run up her spine. The weaving of their lives together had begun to come apart.

Gerran felt the comforting warmth of her body in his lap, yet it was also cooling and turning to a stone that he knew could crush him. He tried to hold onto her, but Darsa got up and went into the kitchen, leaving him in his misery.

In the kitchen, Darsa burst into tears. What had happened? How could such excitement and joy in their lives together suddenly be gone? The knowledge of another being coming into her life was still a miracle, but the consequent responsibility took on new weight. It was a time when she most needed support.

Gerran followed her and tried to console her by putting his arms around her. He was so tired, physically and emotionally, that all he could think of was to urge her toward bed, and to tell her he hoped everything would be better in the morning. As soon as he got into bed Gerran fell fast asleep, but Darsa lay awake for hours beside him.

Gerran was ill prepared for parenthood. As a child he had received virtually no love, so he had never learned how to give it to others. Even with his siblings there were few chances for any kind of close feelings. They ate in a hurry and were sent out into the fields to work all day, except for short breaks to munch on pallas or whatever was ripe at the moment. Dinner at home in the evening was taken up with lectures by his father on how to farm, what each of them had done to displease him, or on what was expected of them the following day. His mother had always been relegated to the background, to serving the family and working ceaselessly, so that he felt he had hardly known her at all.

The closest he had come to understanding love's meaning was when he'd rescued Sril from her plight in the tree. At that moment a small blaze had flamed in his heart. It had flickered and nearly gone out many times since then, but somehow once it was lit, he had instinctively known its value, and the embers had never completely been extinguished.

Unfortunately, he was not sufficiently aware of it to allow Darsa to fan those embers into flames. His relationship with her was comprised primarily of physical attraction and loneliness, and of her willingness to work with him and for him, but that was not enough. Instead of thinking about her welfare, he had remained a little boy, begging to be picked up, not realizing that it was time for him to pick up others when they needed it, and to stand squarely on his own feet.

Darsa herself had also not learned many of the lessons that life inevitably brings to most people. Being an only child, she had been able to captivate her father by doing little more than just smiling at him; carrying the burden of a bedridden mother had increased her closeness to him. She had felt love for Barse, who was a caring father, kind and gentle with her, but her love for him had been tarnished by her proclivity for manipulating him to get what she wanted. He had nearly always responded just the way she hoped he would. She was his "angel child" after all. These same tricks never worked with Gerran. They only confused him and left her disappointed and angry when he didn't respond as her father had done.

Alda, her mother, had been mostly focused on her own often imagined pains and constant wants, and gave little to her daughter other than directives for cleaning, cooking, and errands. But Alda was not an unloving woman. Before her illness she had had many friends, and had often helped those in need, but her preoccupation with herself as she became more attached to her bed didn't leave much room for reaching out to anyone else.

So neither Darsa nor Gerran had much in their own lives to bring them closer together now.

When Darsa woke the next morning, she realized that Gerran had left without waking her. Then Philia's words came into her mind. "The contemplative elders are to be consulted."

Maybe they will help me, she thought to herself.

Chapter Seventeen

Τ he unneeded upper rooms of the schoolhouse had been made into a comfortable haven where the elders kept one another company. They were always glad to accommodate those who sought their wisdom.

"They will know," Darsa thought. "I feel lost and confused, so I'll go to them." She put on her favorite bonnet and started out to see the elders.

In the six months since their giving, Gerran and Darsa had been so busy on the farm that they had only gone to Jom's when they required items that the farm did not provide and when they took their produce there to barter. They had only taken the time needed to make their transactions, and greeted Jom just for that moment. As a result, they were hardly aware of what was going on in Dream.

Dream had become a very active meeting place for many of the residents, and their fellow Dreamians were learning all they could about the Prophecy. They had taken seriously Philia's prophetic words that no one would survive if they didn't learn its message, and each one attain their Eclady. Her monthly visits, which Gerran and Darsa had forgotten about in their busyness, had galvanized groups into action. Between times many were making expeditions into the mountains, looking for Trera's fabled pink stone, the Rock of Knowing, but it had not yet been found.

Darsa walked into the schoolhouse and climbed the stairs to Crone's Heaven, as some had named the room of the elders. Gerran's distressed face kept appearing in her mind, and the goodness in her nature rose on his behalf. "Poor Gerran," she thought. "I was hoping for too much from him."

The door was open, and five pairs of eyes belonging to five lively, elderly women, met Darsa's as she entered. "We were expecting you," they said in chorus, their voices ranging from high soprano to bass.

"I'm Golo's Aunt Fado," said the smallest woman, who had the highest voice. She was wearing clothes of brilliant colors, greens and reds and blues, all of which shimmered when she moved.

Next to her was Laif, tall, slim, and dressed in black. Her voice was a caressing song. "I live in a room that Jom has fixed for me above his store," she said. "My given died during the plague, and I'm very grateful to be in this community."

The five women were seated in a circle, all working on a quilt that Darsa thought was the most beautiful thing she had ever seen. It was made of *sela,* soft and silky yet strong and enduring, and each of the crones was assembling her individual piece. "Unity in diversity," Caal, the merriest and plumpest of the group said, quoting from something she had been told came from the Outside. She was swathed in pinks and blues of many hues.

Each piece of the quilt was a delight to Darsa. Some pieces were in the shape of birds, fishes, flowers, and various animals, and some looked so real that Darsa wanted to pet them or pick them or take them home to play with.

She was enchanted, and almost forgot why she was there, when a flute-like voice said, "Darsa, I'm Gara. I'm a cousin of Drinney's, and I want to introduce you to the quietest one of us all, Mytil."

Little Mytil, wearing garments of deep purple, looked at Darsa, still standing in the doorway, and said in a voice like a large drum, "Welcome, Darsa. We are glad to have you here. Please sit with us and we will reflect together."

There was a vacant chair in the circle that was obviously saved for visitors. It was roomy and inviting. The carvings that covered most of its surface fascinated Darsa. The back of the chair looked so like a bird that Darsa was taken aback. Its wings were spread in such a way that they seemed to embrace who-ever sat in the chair. Darsa felt herself drawn into them. When she was seated, the warmth and comfort emanating from the birdlike chair enveloped her and she felt safe and protected.

Fado raised her arm and faint music filled the room, like the sound of trees bending in the wind, water rippling over stones, animals scurrying in their burrows, or the sounds of love and gaiety.

Laif, whose serenity was echoed in her beaming face, said, "Darsa, we know why you are here. You are carrying new life, and Gerran is not pleased, as you hoped he would be."

Darsa sat wide-eyed and speechless, and Laif went on. "Have you forgotten your giving? Do you remember your own speech in which you said that changes in Dream would not depend on the happiness of your giving but on the fruits of it? This is now coming about. You must have patience and learn compassion for Gerran. He is confused and may not give you the loving care that you long for, but he will be there for you as well as he knows how to be. Everything will come about at the right time in the right way, unless someone tries to manip-ulate and impede the process. Do whatever you know you must do, and trust."

To Darsa's eyes, Laif had become more beautiful as she

spoke. Her face had become radiant, and Darsa started to appreciate the mystery and magic of the elders. She sat as if behind a curtain of wonderment, and when the curtain became transparent she began to see in a new and marvelous way. "How did you know? I didn't tell anyone. Even Gerran didn't know until last night."

Caal's laugh was accompanied by the whispered amusement of the others, and Darsa saw how varied and yet how unified the group was. "Let us introduce ourselves," said Caal.

Fado, dark and stately, began. "I direct these meetings," she said, "and Laif organizes them."

Gara, the one with elfin eyes, said, "I envision ways and answers."

Mytil, in her shades of lavender and purple, said in her lowest tone, "I communicate with spirits, but each of us is completely in charge of everything, none above another. We have been given a task that requires us to assimilate all that we are able to of wisdom, wherever we can find it, from our pasts, from that of others, and from the spirits who are here to guide us. Since all is actually One, by listening and spending long periods in silence, we are given all that we need to know. We have known you for so long. Now we will join hands and impart to you whatever you are ready to receive.

"You will go to the place within you, to the place available to anyone who wishes to go to it. When you know it well and trust yourself in it, it will become the repository of all the strength and knowledge you will ever need any time you choose to enter it. It is there that the Eclady takes place."

The music in the room became exotic, like nothing Darsa had ever heard, and an indescribable current ran through her, filling her being. She smelled flowers, heard the cries of birds, and saw rays of colors streaming across her vision. This is so beautiful I'd like to stay here forever, she thought. I don't want to hear anything, see anything, or do anything else, just stay right here.

"Now, now!" said a voice that pierced her composure like a sliver of crystal. "You may bathe in that peaceful pool for a while, but you have questions to ask and we are here to answer them."

A vision of the orchard and a bereft Gerran sitting under a bereft tree came to Darsa. A pile of pallas that he had found on the ground was beside him, and he looked as if he had lost hope. "Why are the pallas falling? Are we going to lose everything?" Darsa asked.

The music grew a little louder, and after a long pause, a voice that sounded more like a musical instrument than a human voice replied: "You know there is not a single happening, either in Hortishland or on the Outside, that ever occurs by accident. The falling pallas are no exception. You and Gerran have been working feverishly on the farm, forgetting that every person in Dream has been exhorted to study with Philia and learn more about the Prophecy. The needs of the farm must be attended to, but they do not excuse you from your accountability to the community of which you are an integral part. Why were neither of you at Philia's monthly visits?

"As to how much you will lose, that will depend on both of you. You must see your lives as part of a much larger scheme and live them accordingly. You *and* Gerran, no matter how he feels, are bringing a new being into Hortishland, who will have a part to play at least as important as any other Hortishan's. Your child may be a sorely needed link, upon whom the success or failure of the future for all of us could depend. We are all linked to one another and need to become more aware of it."

Darsa thought, I feel everything changing, with new thought and new action. Her heart fluttered, and a small voice within her said, "I am your son, trust me."

The music was carrying her higher and higher, swirling and flowing. She opened her eyes and it took her a moment to recognize where she was, but the loving looks that she received held her in their spell and gave her great comfort and solace.

She smiled glowingly. "I'm glad I came," she said haltingly, as she emerged from deep absorption. "I'm very grateful, more than grateful, for your wonderful caring. My life will be different, and I will know your presence every day in whatever I'm doing."

Darsa hated to leave the wise ones, but one by one, they put a hand on her shoulder and smiled. She bowed her head to touch each of theirs in deep respect, and departed down the stairs of Crone's Heaven.

Chapter Eighteen

*T*he staircase received Darsa in a new way, as if the leaden shoes of her ascent had sprouted wings; coming down, she felt as if she had become as light as dandelion fluff. As she floated down the stairs she saw Drinney coming out of a schoolroom. "Oh, Drinney," Darsa cried out, and continued down the steps to where her friend waited.

"As always, you look so well, as if you'd just discovered a great secret. How wonderful to meet you now! We've been so busy, I almost forgot about everyone and everything, but you know you are always with me. I've wanted to help you here at the school, but I think the farm is devouring me. How is teaching going, and what do you have to tell me? I have so much to talk about with you I don't know where to begin."

Drinney wrinkled her nose in amusement. "Darsa, dear Darsa," she said. "You never seem to change; so much energy, going so fast." She took Darsa's arm in hers and the two young women walked down the road together.

"Everything's fine for me," Drinney said. "The people of this town are wonderful. Many of them are supportive in all sorts of ways, and I have helpers whenever I need them. But I've missed you, too. There's a lot going on. Darsa, have you and Gerran forgotten Philia's request to meet with her once a month? Almost everyone has come to our monthly meetings and we have often wondered about you and Gerran, but Philia said not to bother you." Drinney looked a little embarrassed, and Darsa looked astounded.

"This may sound crazy," Darsa said, "but I think I've been unconscious of anything except the chores I've been doing on the farm. It feels as if I never sit down for as much as two minutes, and it being harvest time now, we haven't had time to think or talk about the plague. I don't know what I'm doing. Oh, Drinney, I haven't even told you the most important piece of news. It's been so long since I've talked with anyone in town."

Drinney took Darsa by her shoulders and, laughing, held her gently. "Calm down, Darsa," she said. "I'm eager to hear your news, but you're wound up like a spinning top, and I can hardly keep up with you."

Darsa looked at Drinney and blurted out, "I'm carrying a new life, but the pallas are falling off the trees. Gerran is at his wit's end and that's all he can think of."

Darsa felt tears coming, and the weight that had been with her on her arrival at the schoolhouse began to return. As she looked into Drinney's eyes again, she saw the eyes of the Wise Women, and felt her true self loosen its wings and shed its burdens. "It's wonderful to have a friend like you," Darsa said. "I've just seen the Wise Women and my life instantly changed from what I thought was disaster to something just right."

"That *is* important news," said Drinney jubilantly. "I'm happy for you, and for me, too. A new baby in the town and a new student for me to teach." She hugged Darsa and danced around her. "How do you feel? Are you excited? You look fine.

"As for Gerran and the pallas, he's not the only one with problems. Others have lost their crops, too. The trees seem not to be damaged, so it's only the fruit. If he had come to hear Philia he'd have known and would have had friends to commiserate with him and to discuss what has to be done. As for the Wise Women, they are our best friends. Each is so different and yet they are all one. We all love them and count on them to share their wisdom when we think we're sinking in quicksand, or drowning, or floating off into space. They are always centered, and they bring us back to where we need to be."

The two women were walking toward Darsa's farm when Darsa awoke to the fact that Drinney was accompanying her, instead of going to *her* house in the opposite direction. "Drinney," she said, "you are a love, but you don't have to go out of your way to walk me home."

"Oh, Darsa, you really have been away too long," exclaimed Drinney. "I live out this way now. I used to live in the country with my sister, Tersa, before the plague, but Tersa was very frail most of her life and the plague took her with all the others who couldn't withstand it. It was an agonizing time for me, as well as for everyone. Then when I got the opportunity to teach school, I found the little house that Toin used to live in, and it is just right for me, close to but not in town, and on the way to your farm. Thanks to the plague, there are a great many empty houses in Dream now. Most are being recycled for elpalm wood and for anything else that can be reused, but this one was just what I wanted and needed and I am grateful to have it.

"You know, Darsa, getting Toin's house has made it clear to me that we truly don't own anything. Everything, even our most treasured possessions, is just on loan, and there's no way to find out for how long. It's a scary thought, but as soon as we see it as a reality it forces us to think in entirely different ways. The way we use whatever we 'have' must be examined in a new light.

"Before, when we've loaned things we've expected them to come back in as good condition as when they went out, and we expected some restitution if they were damaged or lost their worth in any way. Now, if we ask ourselves how we handle what we own from that standpoint, it can be pretty revealing. This is the kind of thing Philia is teaching us, and it's changing our lives. Tomorrow evening she will come again, and I know she'll be glad to see you and Gerran, if you come."

Drinney stopped talking, and turned toward Toin's little house on their left.

Darsa was amazed. She had been so preoccupied with her pain on the way to the Wise Ones that she hadn't noticed anything she passed, but she realized that where there had once been a nondescript little cottage with a messy, neglected yard, there were now varicolored flowers lining a short path to the front door of an inviting house. It had a fresh white front and pale lavender shutters, attractive to passersby.

"Come in and see how cozy it is. We haven't even begun to talk about all the things we need to tell each other," Drinney urged Darsa.

"How I wish I could, Drinney. I'd really love to, but Gerran will be coming in from the orchard very soon, and I want to be there for him. He's been so despondent lately. I'm terribly glad to have had this time with you. You are a great joy to me, and such a good friend."

"I love you, Darsa, and hope I'll see you both tomorrow evening." Drinney held out her arms and the women hugged. That hug gave Darsa the hope she needed for her future.

"You will. At least you'll see me," Darsa promised. "It will be good to hear anything Philia has to say to all of us, and I'm excited about meeting all the Dreamians I don't yet know."

Darsa continued on her way, thinking of what a remarkable day this had been, and of how communicating with only a few people could make such a change in her life.

Chapter Nineteen

The magic of twilight surrounded Darsa as she walked toward what had become her home. A year ago, she thought, I wouldn't have believed anyone if they'd told me I'd be the hard-working given of a farmer, and the incipient mother of a boy, if what I heard in my heart is true. She heard the words again, "I am your son, trust me," and her heart leapt. I have much to be thankful for, she said to herself. As she got nearer to the house, she saw Gerran standing on the porch. He cried out as soon as he saw her.

"Darsa, where have you been? I came home early because there were no more pallas to pick, and I'd done all I could to the garden and the orchard. I thought you'd left me." He was overwrought. His voice had become high-pitched and frantic.

Darsa remembered the beautiful space within her that the Wise Women had helped her access, and immediately she knew how to answer Gerran. Before now, she would have thought he was angry, and in turn would have been angry herself, but from that inner space she saw that what appeared to be anger was fear and vulnerability. "No, Gerran," she said. "I'm not leaving you. This morning when I left here I thought I might, but now I'm back and all is well."

"Not for me, it isn't," shouted Gerran. "Where have you been?"

Darsa climbed the porch steps, and tried to kiss him, but he pushed her away. She started for the door, but he caught her arm and spun her around. "Why are you so calm? Can't you see how frantic you've made me?"

"Gerran," she said, "I haven't made you frantic. You have become frantic with no help from me. I have done nothing to you." She could feel the words coming from deep within her, and she felt that if only he would listen he might understand, but for Gerran this was not a time for listening or understanding. He wanted to make Darsa as upset as he was and it wasn't working. He let go of her and she continued into the house to the kitchen.

She wondered. Was this the Eclady working inside of her? Could it possibly be as simple as that?

As Darsa assembled their dinner of yellow and green kloff patties, and garden vegetables, she knew she was in a state that she had only known for seconds before, and then not clearly. She was surprised that she could feel so calm and peaceful, when the world around her seemed so upset. It was as if a light had been turned on and was illuminating the fact that there need be no correlation between what she felt within herself, and anything coming from outside.

"So this is what being wise is all about," she said aloud to the food that she was putting together. "I can be much happier now even if nothing gets better."

The lesson Darsa was learning was one that every prisoner who is confined for long periods must learn, or go mad. She didn't know that the same condition was true for any who thought they were trapped in some undesirable position, or believed themselves to be victims of any situation. She had found one key to make a less-than-perfect life work.

Chapter Twenty

$\mathcal{T}$he next day, after she saw the Wise Women, Darsa decided to go to town when Philia was there, whether Gerran was willing to go or not. She had urged him to accompany her, but he said that when Philia was near him he felt inadequate. He wouldn't discuss it further. Remembering how Philia had encouraged him in the town square, and at their giving, and how he had responded, this didn't ring true to Darsa, but she didn't argue. She left him hunched down in his favorite chair and left the house.

As Darsa walked back to Dream, she thought how amazingly quickly life could change. There was a great sadness in her heart for Gerran, but the Elders had helped her to understand that all she could do for him was to let him know she cared about him, and then accept that the rest was up to him. He could change as rapidly as she had, but only if he chose to learn and heed what was necessary to bring that change about.

In the warmer months, Philia liked to have her gatherings

outside, but it was getting too chilly to spend much time stand-ing in the cold air, so she had chosen to meet in the annex of the schoolhouse. This was a huge barn that had been converted into a court for games for the children and a meeting place that would hold most of the community. It was heated by the sun during the day, which warmed the south wall, a huge stone wall, and this kept the place warm during the evening. Fortunately, Dream had mostly sunny days so there were not many evenings when the room wasn't warm enough for meetings.

Light in the room was provided by captured sunshine, which gave a special iridescent, warming glow. It was held in crystal containers called *lims*. The lims could be controlled to emit exactly the amount of light needed for any occasion. This was another of Golo's inventions, and the Wise Women were especially capable of seeing that it worked well.

Darsa arrived as the meeting was about to begin, and though the barn was filled, she had no trouble finding Philia. Her lumi-nosity dispelled darkness wherever it was. Moreover, the bright-ness in the room was enhanced by light from the heads of everyone present. Darsa saw the shining lights and felt her own light. The energy coursing through her was very exciting.

Something extraordinary is happening here, Darsa thought. She felt remorse for missing the previous meetings, and won-dered if they had been like this one. It was so intense she was unaware of any individuals, but only of the community as a whole. The Wise Women were strolling among the group, chatting with everyone and giving encouragement wherever it was needed.

Laif, who had summed up Darsa's situation so well the day before, came to her with open arms, greeting her with pleas-ure. Darsa and Laif brought their heads together and exchanged energy. "You heard what we said and applied it," Laif said. "We're sorry Gerran isn't here, but we're delighted to see you. Come with me to Philia. She's been looking for-ward to your presence."

Just then Philia called out. "Welcome, Dreamians. This is an especially joyful evening. We have in our midst our given with whom we celebrated nearly seven months ago. She is with child, a portent for the Dream of the approaching new future. Three other new births will take place in Dream this year, and each will bring us nearer to Eclady, the time of realization. You will make it come about if you live wisely, but for no two of you will it be the same."

Laif took Darsa to Philia, who embraced her, and the three stood together facing the others. "Let us all welcome Darsa," Philia said. "She is fated to contribute much to bringing about the new Dream. We have now had many meetings. For Darsa's benefit, I will sum them up as simply as I can. Each has been about being awake and aware. Being asleep to each other's needs and to the message of the Prophecy is a large part of what brought about the plague. It is also the cause of much of the suffering in the Outside world. The plague would never have come about if being awake and aware had been a priority for the people of Dream.

"There is music, the music of the eternal, playing in the air and throughout the Earth. It takes the silence of a snail or leaf or fine crystal to hear it, but it must be heard if you are to accomplish your mission and not be destroyed by another tragedy, possibly one even more terrible than the plague. The sound of the music, playing for everyone, is beautiful beyond description, and those who hear it will become ecstatic, but there are almost none who do. There are invisible spirits whispering in everyone's ears, but very few hear them, and then only when they listen intently.

"It's unfortunate so many are inattentive. Most of the time you have many thoughts in your heads, chasing each other around relentlessly. Sad thoughts, angry thoughts, critical-of-others thoughts, superficial thoughts; sometimes deep thoughts and good thoughts, and sometimes evil ones. Most of the time your thoughts are of all kinds of *doing*, but not many are of *being*. Unless you stop the babble, and open your ears, you will only hear static from the chaos within you.

"Flowers, and trees, and birds, and all other living creatures, even oceans, and rivers, and mountains listen intently. They grow, and respond to the instructions they hear, and unless obstructed by humans, fulfill their potential. But you, who are able to know and understand all that you need to know, plug up your ears with thick wads of trivia, globs of self-flattery, and messages that come not from your truth, but from the confusion of your own minds. You must learn to revere the wonders of awareness and become fully awake.

"To be true to your mission you must find ways to overcome the state of befogged trance that threatens to overwhelm humanity. The way to do so is to listen. Listen to all and every one of the Earth's beings, to the elements and the sun and stars. Listen to yourselves, your own thoughts, feelings, and intuitions, to your feet when you walk or run along the road, grass, snow, ice, or fallen leaves. Each has different sounds. Listen to your breath, and to the yearnings of your heart. What do they tell you? Only by listening carefully can you find the meaning of life and what to make of it. When you know and understand, you will begin to see your own unique part in the whole. Then you will be able to follow the voice within you that knows all."

Philia smiled and the room filled with an uncanny sweetness. It was as if the air of every in-breath and out-breath was scented with the aromas of all possible flowers, as if nectar fell on lips and thrilled the tips of tongues. Music, unique to each person, filled each of them. All people could do was clap, which they did as Philia vanished, leaving them to their bliss.

It was still light outside when the meeting ended. Everyone was filled with wonder and left silently and peaceably, each in their own cocoon.

Darsa was hardly aware of putting one foot in front of the other. She only knew she had come to the white wooden gate and that Gerran was waiting for her on the porch. How will he be now?

Gerran, seeing Darsa coming toward the house, took one look at her and knew that in not going he had made a mistake. Here was a new and changed woman, a very different Darsa from the one who had left home only a few hours earlier. Gerran wondered, as he had during their giving, who is this woman I gave myself to? When we harvested the pallas she was shy and sweet and docile, and I felt so strong and important to her, but now she has become the strong one and I feel useless. What has happened?

Gerran came down the steps to her and he saw that the light from Darsa's head was glowing brightly.

The six months that followed progressed at a slow and cumbersome pace, a thick and sluggish caterpillar, making its way up an immense stem, hoping to eventually get to a large and juicy leaf.

As the days became darker it was hard to be cheerful, but Darsa managed to retain her inner peace as she grew bigger and heavier, and the action of the child in her womb, in spite of her fatigue and clumsiness, was comforting. She baked and preserved whatever was available, and made clothes for her baby's debut, and Drinney, when she had time, helped her to get things ready for the birthing.

During those cold winter months, Gerran was restless. Darsa had hoped that he would go with her to hear Philia, and find things to do with Jom and the other men in the village, but it was as if something had died in him. He said he didn't want to see anyone, and spent a lot of time sitting in disconsolate silence. Darsa's lisp that he'd found so charming only a few months before had become irritating, and nothing she did pleased him. The light in his head was dim, only becoming a little stronger when his gardening went well.

One day, he came into the kitchen carrying a ten pound *quirzel,* an unusually tasty kind of squash-like carrot that could be made into pies and soups, as well as into delicious adjuncts to all sorts of meals. Gerran had grown the quirzel in a hidden spot Darsa had not seen, but she noticed the light of his head became suddenly brighter. She was so glad that he could still enjoy something she cooked, that she canned all ten pounds of the quirzel, enough to last for months.

Gerran helped Darsa when he saw she needed it, but there was little enjoyment in their relationship. He raked the leaves, harvested the vegetables, and stored what he could in the springhouse his great-grandfather had built long before Gerran was born. He mended everything that needed it, and did a little woodcarving in his spare time.

Darsa was glad when he had enough to do. It was the only time that he seemed even slightly cheerful. The depression that had felled him during the pallas' blight wouldn't let go of him, and he clung to it perversely, as if it gave him some kind of strength, even as it nearly doused his light.

Chapter Twenty-One

To feel useless or unneeded, to be a drone in a bee-hive where the only hope of being effective and the only reason for living is to be able to fly aggressively and fast enough to claim the queen when she takes off on her nuptial flight, that seemed to Gerran to describe his condition in life. He was aware that he had become the father of a child soon to be born, but he felt like a drone whose use-fulness was over. The drone's life is forfeited and he dies at the end. Gerran felt he was dying, but he had yet to learn how much he, as a father, was contributing to the success of Hortishland's mission.

Gerran's recognition of the wonders of the Earth, of the fauna and flora that he worked with day by day, was keen, but his awareness of what it meant to be human was undeveloped. This stood in the way of his understanding other humans. He did not understand himself or those close to him. His part in bringing a new life into Hortishland did not inspire in him either feelings of excitement or responsibility. He would have liked to play the film of his life backwards, to go back to before the giving, before the plague, and to have the film remain *there,* where he saw his life as having been better and simpler. Of course his mind deleted all the negative qualities of that earlier time, and he did not recognize the positive things that had come into his life since then.

As she walked toward him on the path, Darsa was struck by a sense of looking at someone she had never seen before. Gerran's light was faint and he looked sad and haggard. This is amazing, Darsa thought. Why haven't I been more aware? Why has it taken me so long? Poor Gerran! I've had a picture in my mind, ever since we started seeing each other. A picture of my father who waited on my mother until she became so dependent on the spoiling that she stopped doing anything for herself. But Dad was thoughtful and caring with me as well as with her. That was a model that helped me to see how important caring is.

Of course, I was sure I would never allow myself to be spoiled. That was just my mother's weakness, and I was sure I was stronger, Darsa assured herself in her thoughts. I was very naive. Well, it's time I realized that Gerran isn't anything like my father, yet when he was standing on the stage in the square after he and Jom got back from helping the plague survivors, it felt to me as if he were taking care of everyone. Maybe it was the excitement of speaking to a crowd at a moment of unprecedented importance, plus Jom's support, that gave him what seemed to me to be authority and compassion. It's possible that deep within Gerran those qualities are there and available. He doesn't know it now. I will have to draw them out, not by being angry and shrewish, but by being the person for him that I have been expecting him to be for me.

As she climbed the porch steps, Darsa continued to ponder about Gerran. Under the iron will of his father, he never had a chance to express himself, never found out anything about what he might want or need. He is not in touch with himself at all, Darsa thought.

When she got to the top step, Darsa looked intently at Gerran and gave him a warm caring smile for the first time since she'd told him she was pregnant. Now she was big and cumbersome and her time to deliver was fast approaching.

For Gerran, her smile was like a precious ointment. He felt it seeping into his wounds. The terrible hurt of the communication breakdown between Darsa and him had widened the cracks made by the lack of love in his childhood and the frustration of not knowing what to say or how to act.

Gerran had never expressed his feelings to anyone, other than to charge out of the house when his father was demanding. Then he had vented his anger by beating up on nature and his body, digging holes twice as deep as requested, chopping wood into smaller and smaller pieces, or running into town with whatever he'd been told to deliver. With his mother, Gerran had shown glimpses of his feelings by bringing her flowers and the best lagers, pallas, and brins from the garden, but he'd received so little appreciation for these gestures that it was hard to know if she cared.

He needed no angry tactics to appease Darsa. Yet she had not been disposed to accept his offerings from the earth as signs of caring. She took it for granted that since she prepared and cooked the foods, it was just a trade-off when he provided them. He knew of no other way to show his appreciation, so he spent as much time as he could in the orchard with his sick pallas, coming home only when it became dark and he couldn't find a reason to stay out any longer. Then he'd come to the table, wolf down the meal that Darsa had prepared with long-suffering patience, and rarely say a word of appreciation. He'd finish eating and sink into his chair in the sitting room until he was overcome by sleepiness.

At that point he'd climb the stairs and collapse into bed, not even saying good-night to Darsa. She would clean up after him, climb the stairs noiselessly, and get into bed next to an unresponsive lump. The next day, he'd leave at the first sign of dawn, before she awoke.

But now . . . Maybe there could be something between them. She'd smiled at him! She'd smiled as if she didn't hate him, Gerran mused. He wanted her to know that he cared about her, but his awkwardness returned and he merely held out his arm. Darsa took it, and they walked into the house, arm in arm.

Chapter Twenty-Two

For Darsa, the days and weeks that followed were brighter than the previous ones. It felt to her as if the windows of the farmhouse had been thrown open to let in all the powers of the sun and to increase her view of everything growing around the house. The light seemed more cheerful and soothing.

Gerran, whose pallas had stopped falling off the trees, could be heard whistling at his work now and then, and he was more appreciative when Darsa put her delicious lager stews or brin pies on the table.

Drinney was becoming part of the family, with Darsa most evenings. Being together energized both women. For Darsa, it was as if she had acquired a wonderful sister who shared her thoughts and helped her when she needed it. For Drinney, it was a joy to know she was needed and to give Darsa support that was so appreciated. Much of their time was simply enjoying each other and laughing at things. Gerran seldom joined them and was apt to spend the time sitting in his chair feeling rejected.

Sometimes Drinney spent the night, and as the time for Darsa's delivery drew nearer, she moved in. There was plenty of room for her in the big house and there was no easy way to let her know the birthing time had come other than by going for her in the placyl. So it was better for her to stay in the house while they waited.

In preparation for the birthing, Drinney went to see Calile and Cassa and asked them to come by the farmhouse early every morning before they started work. She wanted to make sure she would have their help if it were needed. Everything and everybody was ready, waiting for the big event.

They didn't have long to wait. At three o'clock in the morning on a day in the month of Crant, the moon was shining into the couple's bedroom. Darsa had been sitting up in bed feeling her contractions advancing and receding for an hour. She felt a power and sacredness she had never known before. She wanted to savor it, alone. She sensed that there were beings all about, but no matter how quickly she turned her head or how keenly she listened, she saw and heard no one. Even so, feelings of magic and mystery surrounded her.

Her contractions became so strong she couldn't discount them, and even though they were becoming regular, she didn't feel any urgency. Darsa closed her eyes and sounds of ethereal music, reminiscent of what she had heard with the Wise Women but even lovelier, engulfed her. The music filled her with peace and strength, and she bathed in it until the pains began to intensify.

It was becoming apparent it would be wise to have others with her. Darsa opened her eyes and saw Gerran still asleep, like a child curled up in a nest of covers lit by the moonlight. "Gerran," she whispered. "The time has come. Please go and tell Drinney I need her."

Gerran groaned and snuggled deeper into the covers, "Go back to sleep, Darsa," he murmured, covering his head so that he could neither see nor hear, but Darsa prodded him, laughing to herself, until the pain reminded her there was no more time to play. She pulled off his covers and said a trifle sternly, "Gerran, wake up, I'm in labor. Drinney needs to know it right away." Being her first birthing, Darsa had no way of knowing how soon the birth would happen.

Gerran jumped as if hit. He was standing by the bed, groggy, and didn't know how he got there. "Darsa, what's happening? Are you all right?"

"Of course," she said. "I'm fine, but the baby wants to be birthed. I could have let you sleep, and gone for Drinney myself, but you will need to work together, and I thought it would be best for you to waken her."

Darsa stopped talking for a few moments while the tide of a strong contraction flowed through her.

Gerran became galvanized into action and tried to do a hundred things at once. "I'll take care of everything," he kept saying, as he put both feet into one leg of his trousers. Darsa managed not to laugh, touched by his eagerness and ardor.

Just then there was a knock on the bedroom door, and then another knock. Darsa opened the door and there was Drinney, excited and questioning. "You were talking so loudly, I was sure something must be happening," she said. "So I got dressed and here I am. What's the story, Darsa?"

As if in answer, a long, hard pain took all of Darsa's attention. "Our son is on his way," she replied when the pain ebbed, "and I am very glad you're here. Oh, Drinney, I'm scared and excited and happy the time has come." The two women embraced as well as they could and got ready for the event.

Drinney and Darsa had prepared everything so carefully that Drinney was able to give nearly all of her attention to Darsa, to hold her hands and encourage her as the labor progressed. Gerran wanted to help so much that it was all they could do to keep him busy so that he wouldn't drive them both crazy. They had trained him to help Darsa with her breathing when she required it, and they let him know his part was important, too. When they needed a break from him, they sent him out to gather fruit and vegetables.

As the seemingly endless hours progressed, Darsa still had little time to think. Just as she would relax, another contraction would begin and build so that she felt as if every bone in her pelvis were being torn apart. Just as she thought she couldn't stand this another second, the pain would retreat. But even in some of the hardest moments, she would find herself in a space unlike anything she had ever known, a space where everything became one—the farm, Gerran, Drinney, sky, Earth, and all that grew and lived on it.

The song of life played its melodies. All was one, especially the baby, who was coming into her world through her. When she heard him tell her that he was her son, she named him Larso. The baby was in the center of her space, and all the others there knew that his birth would have a profound effect on all. They were in what felt like a soft, warm, cozy sort of nest, which held them in great honor. It was something Darsa knew, but could not describe. At the same time she found herself high above it, looking down on the nest, and saw it was in the heart of a flower that was very slowly opening petal after petal, allowing more light and air to fill it and enhance its color.

During those periods when Darsa was in that space, she was unreachable, and those who were with her could see everything change. Drinney, constantly scrutinizing Darsa's every move, saw her eyes lose their focus, and, knowing that her ministrations could no longer be effective, became aware of the love and compassion she felt for Darsa welling up within her, accompanied by deep feelings of helplessness. Darsa had slipped out of her care, and was on her own, in the hands of the invisible beings whose presence they all sensed.

At eleven o'clock that night, after twenty hours of labor, Larso "came through," and Darsa, exhausted and triumphant, lay joyful and in wonder.

Drinney held the baby up in celebration, and then placed him at Darsa's breast while she allowed the placenta to drain any lingering nutrients into him. Then she cut and tied the cord while she recited the Hortish Mantra of Greeting.

Gerran was holding Darsa's hand, overwhelmed with admiration for her, and feeling, as usual, his own inadequacies. The sight of Larso, red and squalling, was no thrill to him; in fact he felt an uninvited rage well up inside him at the intrusion of this small being as one who was responsible in Gerran's eyes for Darsa's pain and travail. It never occurred to him to think of his own responsibility for the baby's presence.

Calile and Cassa had arrived early in the morning, both having had the premonition that the birthing was imminent. They stood by the bed, delighted that all had gone so well and that they had been able to support Darsa. They had helped through the long day with cool cloths for her forehead, with rubbing her back, and giving sips of soothing drinks. A bond had grown between the four women that would never be broken.

The Mantra of Greeting, as Drinney recited it, seemed to gather them all in its spell. Drinney spoke slowly and softly.

"I now sever you from the source of life that has been yours for many months, and in doing so I bring you into the world of the All in the One, the One in the All, to whom all nature sings, and I pass to you the power to connect with a new cord of autonomy that will bind or release you. You may let yourself be tied into knots of ego, or you may sever them, if that becomes your wish. You are hereby made able to discover and choose true freedom, to grow and enhance it in yourself and others, or to destroy it.

As Drinney pronounced the last words, a wonderful light shone on the infant and filled the room. Philia appeared, and taking Larso into her arms announced in clear melodic tones *"Til Wan Keil,"* a phrase no one knew, but one that burned itself into each heart.

Hortishland

Standing by the bed, Gerran saw no light, no Philia, and he heard no words. All he heard was the wail of a "newly come" child, and he didn't like the sound.

Chapter Twenty-Three

*L*arso was a colicky baby, and during his first three months he cried a great deal. The sound of his crying irritated Gerran. He tried to be helpful to Darsa, but when he'd hear the constant wails of the, to him, unwelcome intruder, he'd want to head for the orchard, his refuge, and he usually did.

For Gerran and Darsa, after having begun together with an abundance of everything they needed, scarcity had become the order of the day. The slow withering of the pallas took Gerran back to the terrors of the plague, and his mind filled with questions of how to find enough to feed and support the three of them, even though the child he had not expected or wanted was nursing and had need only of the love which he was not willing to give.

These questions assumed unwarranted proportions for Gerran, as he projected them far into the future. They became monsters of fear that overshadowed their lives. For Darsa the fear that consumed Gerran seeped into everything she did and said, and blighted their already rickety relationship. It also wound its tentacles around Larso, who spent much of his time in the beautifully woven basket that Darsa had fashioned for him out of wisteria vines.

Darsa found herself busier than ever, learning how to care for her first child and how to alleviate difficult situations with Gerran. It became apparent to her how quickly farm life could fluctuate between times of feast and famine.

After many months of struggling to save the pallas, as soon as Gerran became resigned to what he thought was a catastrophe, the brins did better than ever before. A new fruit that they called *crilts* appeared out of nowhere in the garden and became the town's favorite gift of nature. They were so popular that Jom was constantly asking Gerran to bring more of them to his store, It was hard for him to make the adjustment, but once again the farm had become as productive as it ever had been.

Meanwhile, Larso grew rapidly and was soon crawling. He was a very active child and his curiosity was boundless. Darsa was delighted with his progress, though she couldn't leave him alone for any time at all. When she had work that took all of her attention, she would sometimes have to leave him with his father. Larso usually cried, but Darsa always hoped that something would spring up between father and son that would erase Gerran's animosity, and that he'd become less gruff and impatient with the baby. For her, Larso was so miraculous, so wonderful, so gentle and sweet, that it was impossible for her not to believe that Gerran, given enough time with him, would come to see these qualities, too, and allow seeds of love and delight to sprout and bloom in him.

But even when he was very little and still crawling, Larso was fearful and would try to hide. In the room where his father liked to sit he had a favorite chair with arms and legs carved to look like the claws of a wild beast. The chair had a skirt that hung from the high seat to the floor and came down on all sides. It was made of the soft velvety leaves and vines of the *cleko* tree. When Larso crawled under it he could not be seen by Gerran, and he imagined he was a griffin in its lair. There he felt brave and strong and fierce, instead of little and helpless as he did when he thought Gerran could see him.

In spite of the pain and confusion around him, Larso grew well and was a bright, healthy child. Before he understood which things were acceptable to play with and which were not, the things that looked most interesting to him were apt to be things that his father had left lying about, such as a revered clay pipe made by his great-grandfather. When his treasures were damaged or destroyed, Gerran found such behavior unforgivable. No matter how Darsa explained that Larso wasn't *trying* to do something to *him,* his anger got the better of him, and spilled over to almost anything Larso did.

For a while Darsa tried to go to town once a month when Philia was there, and when she succeeded she was able to rise above the pressures at home and get back to her own self. But whether out of jealousy or a desire for power over her, when Gerran saw the glow that shone in her after each trip, he forbade her to go to town any more. To make sure she wouldn't disobey him, he said that actually she could go, but if she did, he would keep Larso, and would not let her return.

Under the strain of such restrictions, never thinking of defying Gerran, and with the endless work and her fear of his behavior with Larso, Darsa's thoughts of Philia became obscured, and she put the monthly meetings out of her mind. The advice of the Wise Women helped her cope from day to day, so nothing was really lost. Darsa was not happy, but her true self was only hibernating, not dead. She remembered the Wise Women saying that to move from ordinary self to true self is what Eclady is about.

One day when Larso was almost two, and Darsa was big with their second child, she and Gerran were making a tour of the farm, and admiring how well everything in the garden was growing compared with the years before. Larso was toddling around with them, and on that day, he was irresistibly attracted to a bright yellow flower. With his agile little hands he picked it and gleefully gave it to Gerran. Unfortunately, it was from a special brin plant that Gerran had been nurturing for months, the only one that he had had hopes of hybridizing. When he saw Larso coming toward him with the flower, he saw only that those hopes were shattered. He picked the child up and thrashed him.

With that thrashing, what little trust Larso had in his father was badly damaged. It would not be until he was a grown man that he could look at his father and see anything other than a menacing giant, someone to be avoided whenever possible. Darsa took the child from his father, and with both herself and Larso in tears, ran to the house, while the snake of Gerran's despair encircled his heart in ever-tightening coils.

One day shortly after that, when Darsa went out the back door to call Larso to lunch, she didn't see him anywhere, even though two minutes earlier he'd been playing by the stoop.

He'd never gone far before, and she began to worry. "Larso, where are you? Answer me." Suddenly she saw the child just a few feet away. He was sitting under a bush having a conversation with a stone in his hands. The stone did not appear to be unusual. It was round and smooth like those on a pebbly beach, just the right size to fit into Larso's finely shaped hands, but as he talked with it, in a language Darsa had never heard before, the stone responded to each word he uttered by changing its color ever so subtly. The joy and reverence in Larso's face was beautiful to behold, and the light on his head was brightly lit. The word "Eclady" rang in Darsa's ears. Could this be the freedom that Philia had spoken of, the freedom from the webs of "dos" and "don'ts" that enmesh so many Outsiders and turn them into robots?

She tiptoed away, knowing that the sustenance Larso was receiving from his experience was far greater than anything she could feed him. She realized more surely than ever that as Philia had said, she was entrusted with a very special child.

Chapter Twenty-Four

When Larso was little more than two, an event happened that changed all of their lives. Gwileth was birthed!

The saying has it that "time and tide wait for no man," but now and then someone leapfrogs time, and brings in a new dimension. Gwileth was one of those someones. She was little and delicate, but when you met her, something subtle met you, and you'd know instantly that you were in the presence of a wondrous, ethereal dragon. The fire from its nostrils flared into rainbows of light, and you would have to blink, and blink, and blink again, to get back to the little girl this dragon inhabited. Gwileth's dragon was an expression of her spirit, a wonderful imaginary being that appeared to those who were open to looking at more than her exterior. Larso's griffin was similar to Gwileth's dragon.

In Hortish, Gwileth means "beloved," and this special little girl was well named. She was born at a time of hope, in contrast to the first years of Larso's life, when Gerran had felt that without the pallas, they were close to losing their farm. Now they were experiencing a time of bounty, of having more than they needed.

Gwileth was one of those babies born perfect in every way. Her skin was the color of coffee with just the right amount of cream in it. Hortish genes are diversified so that any appearance is possible in any family, even different-colored skin. Her eyes were slightly slanted and lavender/green, and her hair was taffy-colored loose ringlets. She cooed and smiled at everyone all the time.

Drinney, Cassa, and Calile were there for Gwileth's advent, just as they had been for Larso's. They had become midwives for Dream. This "new lifing" was much easier for Darsa and took only half as long as had Larso's birthing.

Drinney had done the ritual of separation and completion when she cut the cord, and Philia had appeared, as expected, but still unbeknownst to Gerran. She had blessed the child, and holding her high, had proclaimed, "This child will be a model for all who wish to have peace and love in their lives. Eclady is already with her. Observe and learn from her." As she said these words, light shone from Gwileth's eyes and thrilled them all. Even Gerran had been beguiled by this, though he had not seen Philia.

This time, when Darsa had told him she was with child again, Gerran had not been as upset, and she had had the happiness of being with her old friends during her "becoming" and birthing. It had been a renewal for her to be with them, and Gwileth's happy nature, in contrast to Larso's colicky wails, helped to buoy Darsa's spirits whenever her life seemed difficult.

Gerran learned quickly and responded well to his role with the birthing team, and for moments during the hard parts, his compassion surfaced enough for him and Darsa to heal some of the terrible lacerations that had been destroying everything between them.

The trauma he had felt with Larso's arrival was not there this time. In fact, quite the opposite occurred. As Drinney put Gwileth in Gerran's arms, he felt an unexpected thrill, not unlike that when the first buds on his fruit trees opened into blooms.

But for Larso, a different picture emerged. Barely more than a baby himself, it seemed to him he was being rejected and abandoned. His mother was so busy with the new arrival that she had little time for him. She cuddled and sang to him whenever she could, but as he went through his twos, he was into everything and often most of her reactions to him were "No, no, no, Larso. Don't touch."

His father didn't make things better, either. All too often, when Larso was busily examining something that fascinated him, Gerran would summarily pick him up and put him down somewhere else where there was nothing he wanted to play with. He would cry with frustration and rage; then his father would spank him because his crying irritated him so much.

Life for Larso reached a very low ebb, and he began to hate the new baby who, he felt, was stealing *his* mother away from him. His baby feelings became challenges to becoming mature as he grew older, challenges he had to face and overcome, or continue to react as if he were still the angry little boy every time life did not go the way he wanted.

Larso did not know he was being deliberately tested by the challenges that his father's behavior brought into play. The inner strength with which he was endowed rose up to help him, and he found out from trial end error what he needed to learn in order to become a capable adult.

Meanwhile, one day when he was two and a half, Darsa put Gwileth on a coverlet on the floor and left the room for a few minutes to get some brin tarts for the children. A few minutes later, she heard Gwileth cry, something rare for her. She ran back to find Larso hitting her and saying, "Bad, bad baby, bad Gwiss."

Fortunately Darsa had learned from Drinney not to jump to the conclusion that his behavior meant Larso was bad, but Gerran, close behind her, rushed in, picked Gwileth up, and yelled at Larso, "You little monster!" He patted the child whom he had fallen in love with.

It was lucky for Larso that Gerran wasn't able to punish him at the same time he was patting Gwileth, and that Darsa was sensible enough to take him on her lap, hold him, and tell him a story about a little child who was always getting into trouble even when he was trying to be good. As she rocked him, holding his little hand, she noticed small, strange marks on it. Examining them more carefully, she realized they were tiny teeth marks where Gwileth had bitten him.

Most of the time, Larso and Gwileth played well together. They had a natural affinity for each other, though sometimes as they grew older, Larso's need for recognition and power made him forget how much he loved his sister. Then he'd try to lord it over her.

Darsa had become better organized and was free to be with Gwileth more than she had been with Larso. As a babe in arms Gwileth was especially cuddly and her mother took time to hold her and talk to her and call her loving names such as "my little rose," "my angel," "my precious," and as Gwileth grew, she savored those names, especially "angel."

Gwileth and Larso thrived on the farm. Darsa was a caring mother, working constantly to keep the house in order and feed and clothe them all, but much too often she felt that she had become nothing more than a servant to her own family. She did not blame them, but it often felt to her that they were so engrossed in their own lives and comfortable with what she did for them that it didn't occur to them she had needs of her own. At the same time she did nothing to make them aware of what they could do for her, so she was caught in a trap of her own making.

Gerran kept busy with all the farm's outdoor work, but

was less and less communicative with his family. Even Gwileth began to feel her relationship with him was draining away no matter what she did. Larso's fear of Gerran had little reason to abate. Gerran no longer jumped on him as much, but there was little warmth or appreciation coming from him, and Larso kept out of sight of his father whenever he could.

At nine, Gwileth was working hard at school and learning well, and when she was at home, almost all her time was taken up with schoolwork. She helped her mother in the garden and house, cleaning, cooking, and preserving when she could. Cuddling had become a thing of the past, as had praise, and the use of endearing names. Her mother's affections had become mechanical, as she lived her life by rote. Gwileth still longed for the affection she had known as a little child, and wished for the attention both her parents had once lavished on her.

When Gwileth was a baby, Gerran had been a strong, hard-working man of few words. His feelings ran like a vein of gold deep within the mine of his heart, but they were seldom expressed, other than in his work or in unexpected acts of kindness that often went unnoticed. He had played with Gwileth from time to time, and occasionally carried her in his arms to the orchard when it was warm. He'd hang her on a branch, in a swinging seat he had improvised from the willowy fronds of the *pingar* tree. His heart would open for a while, and he would whistle and sing as he worked on his fruit trees. Gwileth would try to imitate him, making little birdlike sounds, and he would laugh and set her swing going up into the pink and purple palla blossoms, up into a world of mirth and delight. But now that she had outgrown the swing and was independent, Gerran didn't know how to keep close to her.

Meanwhile, Larso, at eleven, was all arms and legs, bump-ing into everything. Even this was endearing to his mother, whose heart he had conquered when she heard him speak while still in her womb. He had become very helpful both inside and outdoors, helping with chores wherever he could.

Hortishland

Yet his father acted as if he didn't exist, and the pain of his rejection was always with Larso. He worked hard and did well at school, and with the help of Darsa and Gwileth, set up a farm stand where he bartered their produce after school. When left on their own, Larso and Gwileth invented many games, skipping and hopping, and swinging from the long, strong vines that hung from their favorite pingar tree, which they also loved to climb. Twigs and pebbles were parts of many games, too.

Chapter Twenty-Five

*W*hen spring arrives in Dream, it is much as it is Outside. Crent, as it's called in Hortish, is echoed in everything in nature. Springs that have long been frozen flow once more and supply much-needed water. Little coiled springs, alive within each living being, start life anew. Nature's springs feed multicolored leaves and flowers ready to unfurl as they have since the beginning of time. Small freshets gurgle out of the warming earth of each Hortish soul, singing songs of joy. Trees display new, tender, lacy finery that changes as we watch with wondering eyes. Their brave fresh starts bring beauty into being.

Gwileth, at eleven, could hardly keep still in school. On one early crent day she felt like a spring herself. She wanted to uncoil and fly into the air. I have to get out of here, she thought. I need to be in the real school of my heart and soul, where I can talk with the earth of which I'm part. I feel it in every inch of me.

Hortishland

The peacock that lived in the schoolyard cried its rasping call. Gwileth heard it asking her to come out. She could stay in the classroom no longer. She raised her hand and excused herself, and Drinney Fisch, seeing through her to the dragon within, nodded her head in assent.

Once outside, Gwileth felt the earth charged with the energy of birth, and with a joy that could not be denied. She set off for her favorite place in the woods, and to a little stream. She had come upon it when she was quite small. Realizing she was lost, she had followed its banks, her tears adding to the water, fear driving her feet, until she came out into the field near the farmhouse and saw her favorite tree, the great pingar, massive and imposing over the landscape.

Later, when she sat at the base of *her* tree, as she called it, she could be hidden from the farm and grownups, and know, without thinking about it, the strength coming from it. It was a strength that supported her, assured her that she, the Earth, and the universe were intimately connected. This knowing had been established in her heart and mind as early as she could remember. The tree never ceased to raise her to greater heights, and she often thanked it and hugged it, throwing her arms around its massive trunk.

Since then Gwileth had returned to the woods as often as she could, no longer getting lost. The spot by the stream had become her favorite magical place. Now, it was crent again and there was no way she would be anywhere else.

In crent, sprouts appear every day and grow into myriad of surprises. Tufts of grasses, different colors of green, delicate flowers—bloodroot, violets, tillias, spring beauties, buttercups, jack-in-the-pulpits, and many other scented blooms special to Hortishland—all were redolent of the secrets of spring and summer, showing their unique beauty.

Sitting in her special spot, Gwileth knew how rabbits must feel in their burrows, cozy and safe. The wind rustling in the leaves whispered to her, telling her many secrets of nature. She watched the busy lives of insects, saw how they contributed to the health of the Earth in their different ways. She became more aware of how everything in nature interacts with everything else in a great dance.

She saw that newly birthed fawns were colored to be protected in their helplessness, how as they got older and knew more, they became able to protect themselves. Then no longer needing the safety of their garb, they would shed it to grow another coat. Gwileth remembered how easily she had been hurt when she was little, and realized how, like the fawn, she was growing stronger and surer of herself. Children and young animals are a lot alike, she thought, and hugged herself, feeling her power growing.

Birds came to her and ate crumbs out of her hand. Squirrels tried to compete with them, but she would scold them and tell them there was enough for all. One day, when she was particularly still, a mother skunk and three babies came very near to her. Gwileth loved them instantly. Their bright little faces seemed to tell her that they trusted her, and one of the babies let her pet its coarse black-and-white fur. Gwileth shivered with delight, and the dragon within her stretched up into the trees and emitted a cloud of steam.

There were also tall ferns in the thick of which she could be hidden from intruders. There she would sit very straight, feeling light coursing through her, into her head, out to her fingers, and down through her toes. If she opened her eyes the light would be almost too bright to bear, but instead of being painful, it soothed and healed her eyes and improved her vision. With her eyes closed, she could hear music from all parts of the universe. She could know everything that she chose to know and see the real value of cares and distresses. Often they were so contrived and artificial that she knew immediately that with just one touch of love or truth they would dissipate.

This must be what Eclady is about, she thought. To me it seems like the feeling of complete freedom that Philia talked about, Gwileth reflected. She said we all need it to truly know ourselves, so that we can live our lives with integrity and compassion.

Gwileth saw Larso struggling to be someone that didn't suit him. She saw her parents so engrossed with their work they lost sight of the importance of their love for each other and their children. Gwileth would hold them in the light that filled and surrounded her and let her love flow out to them.

Before she left her secluded spot, she often took some of the copper-colored fluff on the shafts of the ferns (which is why they were called cinnamon ferns) and put it in her pocket. It was soft and wonderful to touch. The rest of the day, whenever she put her hand in her pocket and felt this softness, she felt her own power and joy return. . . .

Larso was finding it impossible to relate to his father. No matter how hard he tried, no matter what he did, it felt to him as if even his best efforts rubbed Gerran the wrong way. Then when Darsa noticed how hard he was trying and interceded for him, it only made things worse.

At thirteen, Larso was tall for his age, lithe and wiry, and very fond of slicking down his dark hair with elpalm gum. He had keen brown eyes that missed little, and a smile that had a way of beguiling even his most resistant acquaintances. His friends called him smooth, but the boy should more rightly have been called a chameleon. He could wriggle and slip in and out of practically any situation with speed and agility and almost before anyone noticed. He had learned well where the advantages and pitfalls of such behavior lay. It had become the only way that he knew to survive.

At the same time, Larso played with his special knowing. He could no longer talk with the stones as he had when he was a small boy, but he had developed insights that let him know many of the subjects that Drinney taught before she even started to teach them. This gave him knowledge far beyond that of most thirteen-year-old boys.

Drinney recognized this ability and protected him from the jealousy and derision of his classmates by communicating with him telepathically, sending him encouragement, but not praising him too much in front of her other students.

One day Larso didn't come home at his usual time to take the fruits and vegetables and flowers to the stand. Darsa, in desperation, sent Gwileth because she knew their father would be angry when he came in from the orchards at suppertime if no exchanges had taken place, even though, initially, he had little to do with setting it up. It was Larso's job to be there every afternoon after school. He hated to be told to do anything and complained bitterly about having to be there when all of his friends were playing and having fun elsewhere, but he grudgingly complied and usually did well.

Gwileth got home from school earlier than Larso, and when her homework wasn't too demanding, helped her mother pick fruits and vegetables, or did kitchen work with her, but on this day Darsa, fearing that Gerran would be furious if no one was there, sent her to take Larso's place at the farm's fruit and vegetable stand. This was a welcome surprise. Gwileth felt as if she had suddenly grown up, and though she wasn't quick with the transactions, she knew she could learn from the trades she made.

In the meantime, Larso had started toward home as usual. Three of his classmates started with him, but they were going to their favorite climbing tree and Larso longed to go with them. He wasn't well liked by his classmates because he was shy and he tried to hide how different he was, so they never got to know him, only seeing him during the short breaks Drinney gave them.

He never was able to stay late, since Gerran, like his own father had, resented his son's going to school. Gerran thought, Why should I let Larso do things that I wasn't allowed to do?

He only grudgingly let Larso stay through the school day. This was perverse since Gerran also was loath to put his trust in Larso and take him to help in the orchard.

So tree climbing was just what Larso wanted to do that day instead of going back to "the stupid stand to sell vegetables." He walked a short way with his schoolmates and was about to reluctantly separate from the boys and go home, when Bort, his greatest rival in class, challenged him to a wrestling match. He liked Bort for his even-tempered, friendly ways, but working on the farm had made Larso lean and muscular, and he was sure he could be the winner. He also knew that he would be the loser at home if he arrived late. He hedged and suggested wrestling another day, perhaps at recess, but Bort thought he was afraid and started taunting him. This was too much for Larso. I'll pin him down quickly and still not be very late, he thought, and if I get dirty I'll tell Ma I fell off of something. She always believes me.

So the fight began. It wasn't quite the way Larso had envisioned it. The two boys started to check each other out, and it soon became apparent that they were evenly matched. The other boys circled the wrestlers, mostly cheering for Bort, but when Larso got Bort down on his back for a second, they started taking sides. Larso heard one boy yelling, "Come on, Larso!" His painfully shy heart leapt. The proud wild griffin deep within him gave a faint roar and Larso heard it. It was a special griffin roar. Suddenly he felt a strength flow through him. Then with beautifully controlled power, yet with great gentleness, he held Bort down, until he, Larso, was acknowledged the victor. Seeing each other as gladiators, they shook hands. The seeds of a long-lasting friendship had been planted.

Larso walked home with mixed feelings. He knew he'd probably be punished for being late, but his pride of accomplishment and the joy of making a powerful friendship filled him almost to bursting. Yet, as he schemed about what he'd tell his mother and father, there was a whirlwind of thoughts in him chasing each other, and his feelings fluctuated between delight and despair.

Larso had been told by his mother how she had known he was a boy before his birthing, and that Philia had predicted a special path for him. Deep inside he knew that his power was great and that he was going through a darkness that had to be penetrated. It was very painful. Before he could emerge from this darkness, he had to shed the scales of the chameleon he tried to be that since early childhood he had needed for protection, and he had to break his father's fearful grip. He also had to get to know his inner power and magic, and learn to use it for the good of all. He was aware that his gentle strength and love toward Bort were steps toward something that made him feel wonderful, and were better than prideful desires to show his superiority. I bet this has something to do with Eclady, Larso thought. . . .

Gwileth set up the farm stand, just as she had so often seen it done before, and waited for customers. Almost immediately, Mrs. Rimble, Bort's mother, who worked at the village clothing shop—it was part of the general store where she did mending for Darsa in exchange for her purchases—drove up and chose carrots, pallas, and a *calbad,* an especially tasty kind of squash. Mrs. Rimble had always been kind to Gwileth, but today she hugged her and told her she hoped she would barter a lot and do well.

Gwileth was feeling very happy, and had just made her fourth trade when Larso arrived dirty and disheveled, and told her to give him the tradings and get lost. "This is my job," he said, and tried to take over.

Gwileth was about to cry and run away when she felt an inner strength that gave her courage. She said, "Not this time, Larso. You weren't here when you were meant to be. Mother told *me* to do this. I'm not leaving."

Larso, who, in the past, had only occasionally considered hitting his sister, realized that he would never again even think of such a thing. He recognized her power and felt a surge of love and admiration for her rise within him.

She didn't look different, but there was something about her that arrested him and imprinted that moment in his mind for the rest of his life. He bowed to her, astonished at himself, and left to tell his mother a story he hoped she'd believe. He knew it would not be as easy with his father, but he thought that if his mother could be persuaded to accept what he told her, she might make it less difficult for him with Gerran.

Gwileth stood still watching her brother walk toward the house, and as she did so she felt the dragon within her raise its head and say "yes." She heard the sound of giant wings opening and then closing ever so softly. At the same time she saw a light around Larso that told her something was happening within him, too.

Just then Mr. Trune with two of his three children approached the stand. He looked at what was still left, some flowers, brins, and two or three of the new crilts that everyone liked so much, as well as a few pallas, and various leftover vegetables. "I'll take all there is," he said, without examining anything. As Gwileth bagged them, Mr. Trune, looking at her, thought there was a strange glow to her that he couldn't quite identify. He shook his head wonderingly and paid her with some of his raggle-bee honey. Then he and his children drove off in their placyl.

It wasn't yet suppertime, but not having anything left to barter, Gwileth tidied up the stand, put the trades she had made into the red-and-purple bag that her mother had entrusted to her, and walked home, as the last rays of sunlight filtered through the leaves of the tall *emper* trees bordering the road. She was glowing with joy and a sense of accomplishment.

It was a dreary, nearly silent dinner. There was a tight moment when Gerran asked Larso how he'd done at the stand and Gwileth intervened by asking her father how the pallas were doing; then everyone left the table. In the same near silence, it became evident to Gwileth that there was something new and different about Larso. She knew that their confrontation at the farm stand had made a difference, but there was something deeper, more profound at play. It was clear that it was something Larso needed to savor by himself, but she hoped he would share it with her someday.

As Gwileth was helping her mother tidy up the kitchen, she proudly gave her the red-and-purple bag with the nuts, berries, and honey she'd received in trade. Her mother took it, but hardly seemed to notice what a success her first sales had been.

Gwileth saw her mother's weary face, and felt a deep sadness. She wanted to hug Darsa, but she knew her heart was so constricted that a hug might unleash too much pain. It would be very easy to break the shell that contained feelings that Darsa could not admit even to herself. So Gwileth gave her mother a light kiss and went to bed.

Darsa, left alone in the kitchen, said to herself: It's no use. I have no life of my own. I'm caught in a hopeless situation. I'm trapped and can't get out. Tears ran down her face as she finished cleaning. She had reached the depths of her self-pity. Darsa had capitulated to Gerran's will to such a degree, and for so long, that it was as if she had buried her own will under the vegetables in the garden. Whenever that feeble will tried to sprout, she'd think of it as a weed, dig it up, and throw it in the compost heap. Yet this will had many sprouts, and sometimes she was kept busy digging and disposing of them again and again. She'd almost forgotten that she was capable of anything other than obedience.

Deep within she knew better, but when she'd get to the edge of the step she was on (from one situation to the next), the thought of falling off to the next one (which might be worse), made the risk seem more than she had the courage for. So she lived within the trap (of capitulating to Gerran's demands) of her own making, in the "quiet desperation" of many Outsiders.

Chapter Twenty-Six

When one gets to the bottom of the pit there is nowhere else to go but up. The look of love and compassion she had seen in Gwileth's face the evening before had awakened feelings of her own that had been suppressed. The mirror in Darsa that should have reflected those feelings back to Gwileth had become so clouded by self-pity, it no longer returned any image.

"I have died," Darsa said to herself, "and I've blamed Gerran for killing me. Where have I been all this time? My children don't see *me*. All they see is an old drudge."

With these thoughts running through her mind the next morning, she heard a voice that said, "Nobody's going to rescue you." Darsa sat upright with a jerk and looked to see who was there, but she was alone. She realized that she had not allowed herself to even be aware of it, but it had always been in the back of her mind that someone or something would change her plight, that "the knight on the white charger" would come, or maybe Gerran would learn to be like her father, and be there for her and wait on her. It didn't matter that that kind of care, when depended on, might turn her into an invalid, a replica of her mother.

It was clear she had to take the reins of her life into her own hands. She saw herself on the top of a hill looking in every direction. She could now do and be what she liked. There was no need for self-pity. She was *free,* and would never again be trapped. It was up to her to make her life whatever she wanted it to be. Knowing this, her spirit soared.

Gerran had gone out to work in the orchard earlier, so she had time to exult at her leisure. The remarkable words she had uttered at her giving, Philia's many inspirations, and her time with the Wise Women, all began to flood her mind. The children were not yet up, so she went to the garden to get something for their breakfast. I won't say anything about this, Darsa thought. I'll just see how long it takes them to notice.

As she approached the garden, she thought it looked very strange, and when she got near she saw why. The bed where she usually spent a lot of time weeding had gotten out of hand. It was filled with the most beautiful flowers she'd ever seen, not the usual *lilias* and pardias, lovely as they were, but new flowers she'd never seen before. Tall and regal, their outer petals were silky, creamy white, and in their centers were tiny purple tufts and pale pink stamens with slightly darker pink anthers. Their scent, exotic and sensuous, filled and overcame her. What are these? she wondered. They seem to come from leaves that I've been pulling up for so long, and throwing onto the compost heap.

Darsa picked a few of the beautiful *ledlias,* as she decided to call them. The name was that of a mythical sprite that her father had told her about when she was a child. She put the flowers in her basket and filled it with the other copious produce of her well-tended garden. An inner calm held her steady and serene, and she returned to the house just as the children were coming to look for her.

"Where have you been?" said Larso. "I don't remember ever not having breakfast on the table by now." Gwileth saw what Darsa was carrying, and her eyes became wide and shining. "Those are the most beautiful flowers I've ever seen," Gwileth gasped. "Where did you find them?"

Darsa loved it when her children were so animated, and she was glad that breakfast and the flowers were capturing their attention and giving her a little more time to get used to the change that had come over her. She put them to work, letting Gwileth arrange the flowers, and letting Larso put her food harvest away while she prepared breakfast.

For Darsa it was like coming through a secret door that she'd only just discovered, finding herself in a new world. At the same time the dark curtain of her belief that she was a helpless victim, a belief that had obscured all other views of herself, had been removed as if it had never existed. She tried to look like her usual overburdened self, but it was impossible. She wanted to sing, dance, laugh. Surprise and excitement filled her, but as she looked with her new eyes at her obedient, somber children, she thought: They've been caught in this trap, too. I've led the way, and we've all been blaming poor Gerran. . . .

Darsa wanted to savor her newfound freedom alone for a while, and she knew that if she could get the children off to school without their active antennae detecting her excitement, she would have the rest of the day to contemplate the changes in every area of her life and the feelings that had accompanied them. She hoped she might discover what she could do with those changes. She put on her glummest face, and sent them off to Drinney.

Left alone, Darsa thought, I succeeded, they didn't even notice. They only know me as tired and dispirited, and that's the way I've known myself. I can hardly believe that everything—*everything*—a whole life, can be so completely altered. She looked at herself. I even look like a drudge. The excitement began to mount again. She went to her room and stripped off her clothes.

Well, at least, she thought, I've been active enough to still have a slim and healthy body, although after I birthed Gwileth I got a little heavy. She found a large bag and put into it all the clothes she'd just taken off. In her closet were a few things she'd kept from her pre-given days, and she was pleased to find they still fit. She separated the things she liked from those she heard herself naming "toiler garbs," and divided them between the closet and the bag. I'll take these dregs to the exchange shed, she thought. This is the most wonderful day of my life!

Before she knew it, the day had flown by and Gwileth returned home from school. Gwileth wondered who was in the kitchen, and had a sudden fear that something might have happened to Darsa. She went hesitantly in the door and was just about to ask the stranger at the table if she knew where her mother was, when Darsa turned around, and Gwileth saw her "new" mother.

"Oh, mother," she said. "What have you done to yourself? I thought a stranger was in the kitchen and I was scared." Darsa laughed. The sound was nearly as startling for Gwileth as was her mother's transformed appearance. Mother came toward daughter with open arms to hug her, and Gwileth collapsed into a chair and burst into tears. "What's happening?" she kept saying.

"Don't cry, darling," said Darsa, and sat down beside her and held her hands. "Our lives have changed and everything will be different from now on. Tonight, Philia will be making her monthly visit to Dream, and you and Larso and I will be there. You've heard me talk about her, but your father has tried to keep us from going, and I have capitulated. We will invite him to go with us. I hope he will, but we will go whether he does or not. There is much that we need to catch up on. You may have learned some of it in school, but I've been locked in, on this farm and in myself."

Gwileth dried her eyes and looked at her mother. "Why, you're very pretty," she said, "and your lisp has gone. What's happened? I can't believe this is real."

Darsa laughed. "It's real reality," she said, "not the terrible world we've imagined we've been living in for so long. We will enjoy everything in life now, and we'll be kind with your father, but not let him dictate to us any longer. I don't know how I became so intimidated."

They heard footsteps approaching, and Larso came rushing in, only to stop in his tracks in amazement. "Is that really you?" he asked. He stood staring at Darsa and she at him. "What's happened to you?" he asked.

Such a transformation had taken place in Darsa that her awareness had become greatly heightened. She immediately saw that Larso was no longer her little boy. Here was a man who had a presence that she had long known was there, but had only acknowledged to herself for seconds at a time. She remembered that same presence in him at the early age when she had seen him conversing with the stones.

Eclady! she thought: for both of us.

Larso had come upon a mother to whom he no longer felt he had to lie, and with whom he knew he could discuss anything and be understood. Their astonishment was mutual.

Darsa said, "Children, you are on the verge of being adults. A new life is opening for all of us. I can see that you know that, too, and I'm very happy that we can all be a part of it. It's too late to work at the farm stand, so just go put a sign up saying we'll be back tomorrow."

Larso found himself whistling, something he'd never done in the house before. As he started to work on the sign, with the three of them chattering and laughing in the kitchen, Gerran walked in. He looked at Darsa in disbelief and, like Gwileth, wondered who she was. Then something stirred in him and he thought, I've seen her somewhere and she's very attractive—oh, it can't be, but it is!

"Darsa. What's happened?" he asked. "What are you children doing here?" He could feel anger rising in him. I've been tricked, he thought, and they're all against me again. His face became distorted, and he picked up a knife, which he brandished in the air. "What's going on?" he reiterated, and without letting anyone answer, he stormed up the stairs and slammed the door to the bedroom.

Nobody followed to beseech him to come back, as they often had done before. The children helped Darsa with preparations for supper and got ready for Philia's meeting. When the food was ready they called Gerran, and when he didn't come, they started without him. When he appeared a few minutes later, they acted as they would have if he'd been on time, asking him how everything was in the orchard, how his day had gone. Gerran was confused. He kept staring at Darsa, mumbling answers to their questions.

When Darsa said they were going to hear Philia and invited him to go with them, that was more than he could handle. Gerran got up from the table, and banging on it, bellowed, "You are *not* going anywhere and I am not going anywhere either."

Darsa and the children put on their jackets, and each urging him to come with them, walked out the door. Gerran was left in helpless stupefaction, which turned into rage. I am the head of this family, he thought. They can't do this to me. His feelings tumbled over each other in disarray. I won't let them back into this house, he decided, and then realized that his life would be useless without them. He went to bed and tossed and turned all night in distress.

Chapter Twenty-Seven

*W*hile Gerran tossed in his bed, Darsa, Gwileth, and Larso arrived at Philia's meeting just in time. They had been so absorbed in their thoughts as they walked that none of them had uttered a word. For each of them, it felt as if they had arrived almost as soon as they started out.

Most of Dream's people were converging on the school barn, walking briskly and chatting with each other as they entered. Many of them were strangers to Darsa and her children.

The children, when they saw their schoolmates, left Darsa to be with them, and Darsa became ever more aware that the last time she'd seen Philia was at Gwileth's birthing, eleven years earlier.

Across the barn floor Darsa saw someone that she thought looked like Calile, and approached her hesitantly. When she got nearer she saw that she was right, but her friend's appearance had changed drastically. When Calile had helped with her birthings, Darsa had seen a woman who was growing as she was recovering from great pain and loss. Now she no longer had the look of pain. She had become strong, but compassion was evident in her every move. Her smile was radiant and her light was very bright.

Calile had continued to run her herb and flower shop, and it had become a healing place and a haven for many. I wonder what I will look like to her when she sees me? Darsa thought.

At that moment Calile turned and looked right at her. For a second there was no recognition, and then Calile exclaimed, "Oh, Darsa, is that you? I had almost given up ever seeing you again." The two women embraced, and tears came to their eyes. Cassa, who had spied Darsa coming up the road, joined the happy reunion and they entered the meeting together.

Cassa, too, had changed. Work in the bakery and with her children kept her very busy. Her shop had become a gathering place, especially for the young, and she was grateful to be able to give sustenance to their inside and outside worlds.

As they walked into the meeting, Darsa saw Drinney getting everything in order. She was on the other side of the barn, and as Darsa saw her she looked up and their eyes met. Drinney's filled with delight and Darsa's with joy, and without knowing how it happened the space between them evaporated.

Friendship, such as that between Darsa and Drinney, is as tough as a bungee cord, can be counted on never to unravel or break, and won't let anyone down too rapidly. The energy that emanated from the four of them was so powerful that everyone in the space turned to see them. They were laughing and crying and hugging one another, all talking at once, not missing, with love and empathy, the other's smallest changes.

To those who didn't know Darsa, she was a mystery. Even her customers who had traded for pallas and brins and other products from the farm only knew Larso, since his mother rarely came to the stand. They wondered where she had come from and how the shopkeepers and their beloved teacher knew her so well. They watched until the space became radiant, announcing the coming of Philia. She appeared suddenly, standing behind the four women.

When Darsa had last seen Philia, her light had lit up the bedroom as well as Gwileth at her birthing, and had added to the joy she had in her new daughter. But in the barn this night, where everyone had come to learn from their teacher, Philia appeared to Darsa to no longer have light emanating from her; rather she had become Light itself. Darsa could barely look at her and her features were less distinct than she remembered them to be.

"This is Darsa," Philia said to the group, and to Darsa she said, "I was expecting you, Darsa. Last night, which must feel like a long time ago to you, you realized the power and the meaning of freedom. You made a huge leap that took care of all the time you've been separated from the Dreamian community and from my monthly influence, although I have often been with you when you least expected it. The lesson Darsa has learned is one that all who want to live life fully must learn. If it is learned from the inside out, it will be retained forever."

Larso and Gwileth, standing on the other side of the room with their schoolmates, were wide-eyed with all that was going on. When they saw Philia, they instantly recognized her as the lady they had often seen in their dreams. They stood in wonder, feeling that the meaning of their lives was just coming into being.

"True freedom," Philia said, "is knowing and understanding that no one, no human being, is really in control of anything or anyone other than himself or herself, and even then, only to manage his or her actions. Control is the prerogative of the universe, which oversees and determines all. To attain freedom requires that you be clear in your mind. The only restraints to doing anything are the ones you impose upon yourselves. When you don't allow yourself to listen to your innate wisdom, you deny yourself true freedom.

"I know I am telling you something you already know. But very few apply these truths to their own lives. They cower and lie to themselves with statements like, 'He won't *let* me,' or 'I *have* to,' or 'I can't,' or 'I might hurt someone.' But they know the truth is that they are afraid to or they can't face the truth. Those who rely on these lies believe them and tie themselves up in them. They believe them to be laws that can't be broken.

"When you know, without a doubt, that you can make *any* choice at any time, no matter what the consequences, no matter whether others approve or not, and that you can accept the consequences, even if they mean great loss, or death, *then* you are free. Then you have become a responsible human being. Then you will be able to handle *anything* that comes into your life."

Philia saw that there was a lot of shuffling and embarrassed giggling in the group. "That all sounds so easy," one man said. The woman by his side shook her head in agreement and said, "But in spite of all you have told us, we're only just beginning to realize that it's true. It's the only way to live and be really happy."

Philia looked at the group with great affection. "You are learning well," she said. "Your thinking when the plague struck was comparable to that of people on the Outside. You had lost track of *meaning* and were mired in *doing*. Those on the Outside rush about as if they are afraid of missing something special. They need to know it's necessary to go slowly if they want to be human and not ants or bees. Much time has gone by since the plague, and we have come together almost every month. But this meeting is a culmination of all that has gone on. It is a time to evaluate what has been learned. It is now time to find out what you who have chosen to complete the purpose of Dream's existence still need to accomplish.

"I see that my two young charges who have been tutored by Drinney are here with Darsa, their mother, for their first meeting. They have undergone great changes and their lives have been moving toward this moment. Gwileth and Larso, please come here and stand with your mother and her friends who helped her so much when each of you made your appearance in Dream. You have seen Calile in her shop, and Cassa at the bakery, and her children: Milsa; Tas, Jr.; and Nila, who finished their schooling when you were just beginning. I see that Sheil and Brul Golo are also here, and your friend Bort, with whom you tested your strength, Larso. I am very pleased. Gwileth and Larso are brave to come here against the will of their father, as have Sheil and Brul. Gerran and Golo have both elected not to attend these meetings. Golo, with a few of those who are still angry because of their reactions to the plague, has formed a group that is against whatever we stand for."

Darsa thought, if Gerran hears about this he'll want to join Golo, but his attitude and isolation will protect him from ever learning of such a group.

Philia asked the Golo boys (Sheil was 19, Brul 17) to come forward and tell the community why they had chosen to be there in spite of their father. As the young men walked across the barn floor, it was obvious they had learned to rely on themselves and had become self-confident, able young men.

Sheil spoke for both of them. "We were fortunate to have Byphon the cladloc look after us when we were very little, when our father was so depressed he was barely aware of us. Byphon taught us the life within us is more important than life outside us. When he went from Hortishland, he left us the wonderful gift of understanding how true that was." (Because of the plague and the need for Eclady, all Hortishans are more mature, even the kids, than Outsiders. They're searching for the wisdom they need.)

"If you will all sit and get comfortable, Sheil and Brul have a story to tell," said Philia.

"We do," said Sheil, "but how did you know?"

"I am always with you, you must know that by now," said Philia.

Sheil and Brul faced their fellow Dreamians and felt strengthened by a sense that they were part of these people, the family they had always longed for and with whom they could share whatever they chose.

Sheil started. "When our mother died from the plague, our father felt deserted. He was never able to come to terms with his feelings. She had left him, so it didn't matter how or what had caused her to leave, the anger he felt seethed within him. We were three and five then. He hadn't paid much attention to us before, and didn't know how to start. Dad was only interested in inventing. We were noisy and got in his way. Sometimes we boys took the brunt of his unhappiness when we were a little older, arriving in school disheveled and bruised. Everyone in school knew how things were for us, and Drinney, in her wonderful way, used our plight to teach our classmates lessons in compassion.

"We were never teased or picked on because the other children were encouraged to see how hard our situation was through no fault of our own. Byphon contributed the most to our upbringing. He passed on wisdom and patience when they were needed, as well as compassion for our father, who was often irrational.

"At the same time, the power of Dad's anger drove his inventive mind to greater creative heights. He made many improvements in his original invention, the placyl. He invented new gears that made the pedaling easier and increased its speed. He made a way to noiselessly alert others of its approach by pushing a button that awoke the intuitive reflexes of people to its presence. Of course you placyl owners know this. He designed a mathematical machine for Jom that made his accounting simpler, and he made also all sorts of gadgets that most of you Dreamians use every day. Then he found a substance deep in a cave in the foothills of Cranth. In the cave, it was thick and creamy, but when taken into the air it slowly hardened so that it could not be scratched or shattered or damaged. He made many indestructible things from it, coins and medals people wore around their necks or used to play games with.

"One day when Brul and I were old enough to go to school alone, we were nearly home in the evening when we saw a strange large mound in Byphon's field. At first we thought Byphon was playing one of his ingenious tricks on us. Brul said, 'There's something funny in the pasture. What do you think Byphon's up to now?'

"I'd been ambling along, kicking little stones in front of me, and only looking up when Brul distracted me. 'Oh, wow,' I said. 'It looks pretty weird to me. Let's be careful. Byphon's probably hiding behind it, so if he hasn't seen us, maybe we can sneak up on him and surprise him.'"

Brul spoke up and joined Sheil in the narration in the barn. "I was scared," he said. "I got closer to Sheil, ready to be his shadow whatever he did. At times like these it was nice to have an older brother."

"We were whispering then," said Sheil. "Going very carefully, I told Brul, 'You go to the right end of whatever it is and I'll go to the left, and when we get close, we'll make a mad dash around to the other side and scare him.' Brul was jumping up and down with excitement, and at the same time trying to be quiet. 'OK. Let's go.' We crept as fast as we could on hands and knees, hoping Byphon wouldn't suddenly appear and ruin our fun, but nothing happened. When we got to our destination, I signaled to Brul, and we rushed around the mound, yelling and shouting, 'Byphon, we've got you!' But we were running so fast we ran into each other. Byphon didn't appear.

"We looked at each other in wonder, then we looked again at the mound. There were two huge, unusual doors. They looked like wings. We were so eager to see what was inside we didn't take time to look at them, we just saw they were open!"

"'What do you think that's all about?' I asked Sheil. 'I don't know, but I bet it's something Byphon fashioned,' Sheil answered. 'Let's go in and take a peek.'

"I was a little scared, it looked so dark. So I said, 'Sheil, you go first.' He stepped into the entrance and disappeared. 'Come on,' he called back to me. 'Are you afraid?' I had a feeling he was scared, too, but didn't want me to know it. I yelled, 'Wait for me,' and then, as I went in, I let out a shout. It was not dark in there at all.

"The ceiling was made of something translucent. It shimmered and constantly changed colors and lit up the room with a wonderful light. We were thrilled. What was this building that we'd never seen before? There was a line of markings in two rows that went around the room just below the lighted ceiling. It was in characters Byphon had taught us. We started to compete in reading it, then realized that we could do it better together. We remembered Byphon's lessons on cooperation being the best way to make anything work."

"We saw a sign that Byphon often used when teaching us," Sheil picked up the narrative. "We figured it must be a message from him. But where was he? We were getting excited. The first thing the message said was 'Farewell, my friends,' and then, 'I am sad to have to leave you, but the time has come when I am no longer needed here, and other Hortishlands are asking for me. Whenever you need me and call me I'll be with you. Just sit under the glowing dome and you will know my presence.'

"We looked down at our feet for the first time and realized we were standing on a beautiful rug. It looked like a garden. It had all sorts of flowers we'd never seen before, so real we wanted to pick them. They were blooming in profusion all over the rug, except in the very center where there was a grassy spot. That's where we sat. When we were settled, we somehow knew to hold hands and look up. Light from the ceiling lit up our bodies and filled and nourished us. We sat in awe, then suddenly heard our beloved Byphon speaking in a new voice.

"'I am a long way from you, but always with you. My love for you will never leave you, and will permit me to appear to you whenever you come here. I hope that will be often so that I can answer anything you want to know about as you grow up to be the fine men that you are becoming. I made this to be your place of refuge. Use it well.' The light became dim, and then we sat in silence.

"Finally, Brul said to me, 'Do you think Dad knows about this?' I shook myself, wondering if what we'd just experienced could actually be real. 'I don't know,' I said. 'Let's go see. We must be very late and he may be furious.'

"We walked the short distance home; and found our dad standing in the doorway. Oh boy, I thought, I bet we're in for it. It's got to be very late, but Dad was in a rare good mood. 'I'm glad you're home from school so promptly,' he said. 'I have things for you to do.' Brul couldn't contain himself. 'Have you seen what Byphon put in the field?' he asked.

"'Byphon left today. He said he couldn't wait and asked me to say good-bye to you. We will miss him,' said our father.

"'But Dad,' Brul said, 'the mound in the field. Look over there. Have you seen it?' The Bump, as we had named it, stood out against the evening sky, and as we watched it, we saw a tiny spark flash from the top.

"'You're imagining things, son,' said Dad. 'There's work to be done. Come along now.'

"We looked at each other, amazed. Brul winked at me and said, 'OK, Dad. What can we do for you?'

"Thanks to Drinney, we have learned what we needed to learn about everything at school, and thanks to our meditations in the Bump, which Dad still does not see, it has become clear to us that these monthly meetings are where we need to be, to learn what we can contribute to Dream. Thank you."

The boys turned to Philia. "Was that all right?" they both asked at once.

The Dreamian community clapped and cheered until Philia held up her hand and said, "It is a great joy to have these four young people, and Darsa, added to our midst, and now we can inform them of what we have been doing in the last thirteen years, and tell them what we still have to make come about.

"These years and monthly meetings have all been in preparation for the time we still have left in which to finish the work that your ancestors, Cloa and Lomay, were sent here to do, work that was handed on to you to bring to fruition. My role is, and has been, to help you find and map out the road that must be taken.

"For the benefit of the newcomers, I will, as succinctly as possible, describe some of the steps that have been taken. This group, with the guidance of the Wise Women, have come to recognize that everyone here is a unique being, that no one is more important than another, that each has his or her own special and singular part to learn, understand, and use in accomplishing the tasks that are required. The community has also learned that no two Dreamians are on the same part of the mountain that has to be climbed. Cooperation, coordination, respect, openness, and willingness to do whatever is required have brought all of you within sight of the summit.

"When each of you has reached his or her Eclady, the inner freedom that is uniquely yours, you will be ready.

"Everyone is in the process of climbing this great mountain of comprehension, from the crest of which, when it is reached, will be seen all that is needed to bring the Outside world back to sanity, compassion, and peace.

"You, Darsa, as well as your children with you, have been climbing it with us, though you were not aware of it, and Brul and Sheil have done their part, too. Truths to learn and live by have been found at the same time."

Philia looked at the completely attentive group and said, "You all are a great joy, so eager and willing. Dream has always been a beautiful town, but you have turned it into a place of harmony and peace. Poor Golo and his friends must be watched, lest they harm anyone, including themselves, but you have all come to be able to view them with understanding. You realize that the fear and anger they direct toward you comes from the erroneous belief that their pain has been inflicted on them maliciously to make them suffer.

"With your respect and caring, instead of continuing to think they are victims of the town's jokes and humor, as they see themselves now, perhaps you may open their eyes. If you do, I can promise you that they will become at least as eager and willing as any of you are."

Philia looked around the room and all those who looked back at her felt as if they were being filled with the nectar of some exotic fruit, and that it had made them invulnerable.

"At every meeting, from the very first, we have contemplated the Laws of the Prophecy. This month there is one young man here, Cavin Blai," she said, "who has learned the principles of the Laws that all must practice and know so well that they become the only answers to life that make sense to them.

"All of his family died in the plague. He was seven months old when it happened, and Jom, in going back to make sure that all the houses had been visited, found him, weak and hungry. Jom took Cavin to his home above his store and nursed him back to health, and the pain in Jom's heart over the loss of his friend Toin and of the many others who had frequented his store was alleviated by his compassion for the small boy.

"Both Cavin and Jom learned a lot about love from each other, and about life, and have been gratefully living together ever since. Cavin is now fourteen, and most of you know him through his friendly helpfulness when you shop at Jom's."

Philia looked across the large room to Jom, who had just caught Darsa's eye and had smiled in recognition.

To Darsa, Jom looked much older than she remembered, but, of course, many changes can take place in fourteen years.

"It's a pleasure to see you looking so well, Jom," said Philia. "You have become more and more the mainstay of the community, always there to help anyone when help is needed, and so in touch with everyone that you always know who will take care of even the most baffling situations; and you Cavin, my guess is that you now take as good care of Jom as he did of you when you were growing up. Would you be so kind as to recite the principles that you have been studying and have learned so well?"

Darsa said to herself in horror, This will be our first time to hear them. No wonder we've had so much trouble.

"Please come forward, Cavin, and tell these newcomers what they have missed," said Philia.

Cavin Blai, standing in the back, stepped between the people in front of him and walked to Philia, whose light engulfed him. He stood in front of the group, young, strong and with an air of self-assurance that gave a lift to everyone's spirits.

"These are the principles of the Prophecy of Illan that I have learned from Philia at the community meetings," he said. "There are seven of them, and if I forget any of them, the Wise Women help me remember.

"One. Anything that is revered or treasured more than the Light that is within, guiding and showing the way, will lead to disaster. Those who do not recognize that the Light must be paramount for life to have meaning will not know joy or peace.

"Two. What may look like a wonderful gift may turn out to be a very painful lesson. That which appears to be repugnant may be an unexpected, great gift. Learning is one of the purposes of Being.

"Three. Trust in the universe, in the One in All, is the foundation for all the principles; living in Trust brings life into fruition.

"Four. Compassion is the greatest form and the true name of Love. It is unconditional. It asks for nothing and gives all.

"Five. Every being is alone and yet is also part of every other being, as well as one with the Light and the universe that knows all and is in everyone and everything.

"Six. Self-understanding is the foundation of all relation-ships that are viable, satisfying, and successful, because only by knowing oneself is it possible to know others.

"Seven. The good, the true, and the beautiful are three in one. If these are made the choice of enough individuals in any community they will bring joy and peace to all in that com-munity.

"These are the principles of the Prophecy as I have learned them."

Cavin stepped back, and Philia said, "Thank you, Cavin. These principles, if incorporated in a community's everyday life, will enhance the lives of all. They will bring light into the lives of those who abide by them. They will spill over into those whose lives they touch."

This is an amazing evening, Darsa thought. She looked at her children and their rapt expressions. She saw Fado and Mytil off to the left, and noticed that Laif and Gara and Caal were chatting with an elderly woman. She felt infused with energy as she thought how helpful those Wise Women had been in the past and that they were here now whenever any-one needed to see them. Again she realized she was free to choose *anything* at *any* time, and the only person who could deter her was herself.

Philia said, "We now have something special for everyone to enjoy. Dream's wonderful Wise Women have been in seclu-sion, as you, know, for seven days, during which they commu-nicated with the Outside. . . ." She let the impact of this announcement settle on the audience.

"Through their communications, you can know pain and suffering are there. Your attention and understanding will be required. You must hone your lives until your hard-won wis-dom will be irresistible to Outsiders. If they don't learn better ways, they will destroy themselves. Their only hope of survival will be to learn what *you* have learned, what *you* can teach them."

The Wise Women were standing together. As everyone turned to look at them, flashes of brilliant light shimmered around them. Mytil and Fado stepped forward. "We have much to tell you," they said. Their voices sounded like bells tolling, like children crying. "There is more suffering among those on the Outside than any of us imagined. We must keep trying to help them while it is still possible. There will be only a short time to do this. That time will be when enough of the Outside men and women realize they need help and ask for it."

Caal, Gara, and Laif spoke with one voice. "We have not been able to tell you this before because it has only now started to manifest itself as part of the work that must be done by this community. We have been in contact with a person on the Outside. He says he's in a city called New York. He says it is so big and that so many people live there that it would be impossible for anyone in Hortishland to imagine what it's like. He lived in Dream as a child, and does not know how he was transported Outside. He'd like to come back but, as our only contact, he is more valuable to us where he is. His name is Jad. Has anyone here heard of a person with that name?"

There was silence. No one answered. Gwileth went to Darsa and whispered in her ear.

"Oh, yes," said Darsa. "I'd almost forgotten. Gerran, my husband, had an older brother called Jad. He ran away from home, went up into the mountains many years ago when he was a boy. It was before the plague and he hasn't been seen since. Do you think it might be this Jad? We thought that he must have frozen in those cold hills and that he must be dead."

The Wise Women looked at one another with delight. Their shimmering became almost blinding. "He said he was from Dream so we knew we would find his family," said Caal. "Now we'll learn more and be able to communicate better. One day when we were meditating we all heard his voice. It came to us telepathically. It seemed he was just talking to himself and had no idea that we had tuned in to him. We have found we can speak to him in his dreams and listen to his thoughts when he awakens. He is completely unaware that anyone is reading his thoughts, and because they're uncensored, there are times when we feel guilty for listening, and sometimes shocked.

"Jad is as well as most of the Outside people who live in cities. We have been fascinated at how much he can abuse his body yet remain physically all right. He is perpetually breathing in smoke from a thing he sets on fire to produce smoking embers. He calls it a 'cigarette.' Even though he knows doing so is a danger to his health, he finds it difficult to stop. The food he eats is not healthy either, and what he drinks is even worse.

"We are learning as much as we can about the Outsiders through Jad. This way we will find out clearly what our work has to be to keep them from disaster when the time comes for us to intervene. This has been, as Philia told us, the whole purpose for the existence of Hortishland from its inception—to help the Outsiders.

"Jad is providing us with vital information. We have found out a lot more about him, about his adventures since leaving Dream and his yearning to return. We cannot let him do so until our knowledge is greater, because at this time he is our most important link. But someday, in gratitude for his assistance, if we don't join him first, we will bring him back home. If anyone wants to know more about him, come see us, and we will tell you what we can."

Philia spoke once more. "When Jad ran away he provided just what was needed for Hortishland to be informed about the Outside. That's why the All-Knowing saved him from freezing. All that happens is part of a greater plan, as I have often told you. Your participation is needed to have it all go well. A lot depends on how Jad has grown up and what he has learned."

Philia commended the group on their dedication to helping bring about what was needed to save the Outside. "There are several ways of preparation that you have been working on with me," she said. "Darsa, Larso, and Gwileth need to be told of them, primarily about the work you have done with your own lives, getting in touch with your inner selves, becoming able to distinguish them from the outer selves to which you were formerly enslaved. You have made such important changes in your lives. Your understanding and empathy with Outsiders and your patience have been enhanced. Your lights have become so bright that we needed nothing more than them to illuminate this room tonight. I leave you now for another month. Use this time well to share what you have learned."

Philia lifted her arms in blessing, and each Dreamian felt as if he or she were spinning in a rainbow of colors, one that nourished and supported them and filled them with confidence. Exquisite music filled them, and then, as always, Philia was gone without a trace, as if she had never been there.

Chapter Twenty-Eight

*A*s the meeting began to break up, several of the group approached Darsa and welcomed her back. She touched heads with many of them and felt as if she had been reborn into a new life, a life already filled with wonderful, dependable friends, now enriched by potential new friends.

She called to the children to start toward home. They were saying good-night to their schoolmates, all talking at once and enjoying each other immensely. Darsa wanted to stay forever, the evening had been so magical. She promised herself to come as often as she could to get to know some of her Dreamian neighbors and to work with them to bring about what Philia was asking from all of them. She thought that possibly some of the men might be interested in the orchard and might get to know Gerran (a faint hope, she had to admit, but not to be discounted). Mostly, Darsa wanted to see much more of the Wise Women, Calile, Cassa, and, of course, Drinney.

Drinney appeared by her side as Darsa started out for

home, and when the children joined them, they all went down the road together.

Darsa and Drinney looked into each other's eyes, and then Drinney said, "Yes, Darsa, you've finally done it. No more of the skittishness that has given you so much grief and kept you enslaved to all the shoulds and shouldn'ts in your life. You are obviously free. What happened? It's emblazoned all over you, the way you look, the way you smile and talk, and the way you hold yourself. When we walked down this road together after you saw the Wise Women for the first time, you had a glint of it, but it wasn't established. Now it is. You'll never lose it, and I'm very happy for you. What made it happen?"

Darsa stopped walking and hugged Drinney. "Your patience and example, I know, must have had a very big part in it, but it all happened in an instant. Suddenly, I *knew* I was no longer dependent on anyone or anything, and that *I* must be responsible for everything I think or say or do. I knew that everything is part of a greater plan, greater than anything I'd ever heard of, and that everything is right, exactly the way it is, no matter how it feels to me or how I may see it.

"I've been riding on wings that carry me everywhere, ever since this happened. I have no more worries or tension. Oh, Drinney, I love you. You have known this all along and have never pressured me. But you've shown me everything I needed by your example. Thank you so much. You are Love embodied."

Darsa's face was radiant, and Drinney laughed with the joy of seeing how she had changed.

"My children have a new mother and life will be better for all of us," Darsa said.

Larso and Gwileth were still caught up in what felt to them like a dream. They were floating in the excitement of the evening, but their mother's words resonated with their own thoughts. Gwileth told Drinney how happy she was to have her for a teacher, and Larso echoed this. They told Drinney they knew they had work to do and that they welcomed it.

Hortishland

Almost before they knew it, the little group had arrived at Drinney's gate. She hugged the three of them and turned to go home. As they called good-night to Drinney, they felt the powerful bond that held them together, and knew it would always be there. Even if they were separated by great distances, it would stretch itself as far as needed with resiliency and strength.

Chapter Twenty-Nine

The moon came up as Darsa, Gwileth, and Larso continued on their way home. The light was beautiful, shining through the leaves of the emper trees as they approached the house outlined in its light. The magic of the evening lingered with them.

They were expecting Gerran to be on the porch, scolding and angry, when they arrived, but there was nobody there to greet them except Rall, a cuppy of Trad and Cama. Cama was the trog of a deceased neighbor. She had turned up one day when Trad had been dejected, and they had taken comfort in each other at once. Since then they had had three cuppies, all of which delighted Darsa and the children. Cama's presence had been a joy to all of them.

Rall had been sleeping on the porch, but hearing their approach came bounding out to meet them. He was about half grown, and his friskiness matched the joyfulness of the three as they returned home. Darsa and the children felt a little guilty for their relief in not having Gerran there to dampen their spirits.

They supposed he had gone to bed, and they were ready for bed themselves.

Gwileth asked Larso if he'd go with her tomorrow to a place that she had wanted to show him for a while. Larso said he would and was struck by the beautiful glow of Gwileth's light. Of course his own was equally fine, but he didn't know it yet. The three kissed, hugged sleepily, and happily went to their rooms.

Darsa was glad to find Gerran asleep. Stretched out in the bed, she was happy to be able to savor the evening and went to sleep with no recriminations to mar the joy she was feeling.

The next day was bright and beautiful. Gerran was about to go to the orchard when the others appeared for breakfast. Gerran complained that he had too much work to do, and Larso immediately said, "I'd be glad to help. Is there anything I can do for you?"

Gerran looked at Larso with surprise, verging on alarm. "Of course, I could use some help," he said grumpily. "If you come with me, I'll show you."

Gwileth said, "Don't forget, Larso, you've promised to go with me today."

Larso smiled at Gwileth and his mother, and said, "Don't worry, Gwil. When Dad's done with me I'll come back, and you and I will go wherever you say."

Gerran was getting impatient, so Larso grabbed whatever he could carry to eat and leapt to the door. Father and son departed in the closest thing to harmony they had ever known. Darsa and Gwileth looked at each other in amazement and happily watched them go. "Well, we'll see," said Darsa, and Gwileth nodded.

An air of conspiracy was arising between mother and daughter. They knew they both felt very good and wanted to make the most of the time they had together. They cleaned up the kitchen, then went to the garden, which greeted them with the perfume and beauty of the new ledlias and with all the opulence of a well-tended garden.

Darsa said, "We'll have to tell Gerran about Jad and keep in touch with the Wise Women to learn what they are hearing from him. We must find out what part we can take in what they're doing, and help wherever we can."

"Wasn't that an amazing meeting last night?" Gwileth said. "I feel as if you've become one of my best friends. We have *so much* to tell each other." Darsa smiled and hugged her new friend, and the morning flew by on magical wings.

As the young woman and her mother were getting together a meal of pallas and kloff patties, plus a few crilt, Larso came into the house saying that Gerran had told him to come home and that he'd be ready to go with Gwileth as soon as they'd let him have some of the food they'd prepared.

Gwileth and Darsa said together, "Larso, we are amazed by what we have found. We've found that we're free to tell each other about how much love we feel. It is so strong! Why couldn't we do so before? Why did we beat around the bush so much?"

Larso answered, "It's so simple. We've been reaching *out* instead of *in* to where all the answers are." He was beaming. "I've begun to talk with the stones again. And I love you both."

Darsa and Gwileth had only prepared enough food for themselves, but told Larso if he would get whatever he wanted from the garden, they would cook it for him. Larso returned quickly with all he needed, and he told them about his morning with Gerran. "It was strange. Dad hardly spoke to me. It was as if we were strangers. I became tongue-tied. I'm so used to him yelling at me that it all felt unreal. Anyhow, he put me to work on a new bed for crilts. He gave me the hoe and told me to turn the soil over until it was broken up. So I pitched in and did it a lot faster than he expected. When he saw I was done he seemed to get almost angry, and ordered me to leave. He said that he wanted to be alone, so that's why I'm here. I wouldn't have dared to leave until he said I could, even though I wanted to get back to you, Gwil. You can imagine how pleased I was when he said, 'Go,' but I left the hoe behind. What shall I do? If I go back he may decide to keep me there. If I don't, I may get yelled at this evening." Larso looked at his sister and mother quizzically. "What do you think?" he asked.

Darsa glanced at her children and thought: We have all come so far so fast. Nothing unpleasant that happens seems to matter much any more.

"You two go along," she said. "I plan to go out later anyhow and I'll pick the hoe up."

"Thanks, Ma," they both said, and were gone instantly.

Gwileth started toward the woods and Larso realized that, while he had suspected that Gwileth's trips there were more important than he had thought, he had never felt he could go with her. Now he knew that by this trip together the trust between them was being sealed. As they entered a grove of trees, Gwileth took Larso's hand and led him into a thicket where the ferns grew high.

They settled down amidst the ferns, and noticed that each fern gave off a light and warmth that were protective and comforting and that illuminated their cozy space. They sat up straight, and then Gwileth began to sing. "Oh Light, come fill us both. Fill our hearts and minds with Love."

Larso wondered, Is this some sort of mumbo jumbo? But as Gwileth kept singing, he began to feel a tingling rising up his spine, and then he was filled with a deep calm.

"We come to learn the Wholeness," she sang. "The magic dance of the All in One."

Larso felt himself becoming one with everything around him. He saw a rabbit hopping toward him, a turtle, a fish, a flower in bloom, its fragrance filling him with joy. He saw a polished stone encircled with many rings, and he heard it speak. He recognized its sounds and the way they kept changing from his childhood. It said, "We, the foundation of the Earth, are here to support and uphold you. Do not damage our world. Watch where you put your feet and how you step or dance." Then Larso saw butterflies and grasshoppers, insects, viruses, bacteria, microscopic beings, every kind of creature, deer, *chagou,* bear, cladloc, wolf, *chickadal,* and more, and still more. They came to sing with Gwileth: "We are one, one with you, as you are one with us and all others."

Those creatures that were small settled in Larso's lap, and as they did so, he felt them merge with him. He understood the importance of the rabbit's long ears, the squirrel's strong teeth, the fish's scales. He felt himself rushing around with billions of microscopic beings, and realized that nothing could function without them. Their work was incessant, unseen, but critical for the survival of all. Each creature contributed to every other, and when one was lost, those that were left became less than they had been before.

He looked into the eyes of eagles, *stiggies,* otters, skunks, *pagas,* and kangaroos. Each told their story, how they served the Earth, how they were crowded out and made homeless by humans. Larso held out his arms to embrace them, and as he did so they filed into his heart, and in the joy of their presence he cried out.

In her previous visits to her "magical place," as she called it, Gwileth had become filled with all that Larso had just experienced, and she felt his joy as she finished her song. Then she looked into his eyes and saw that he had changed as radically as the frog had when it became a prince. There was nothing different about Larso physically. His hair was still wavy and brown, his nose was as straight as always, and his dark brown eyes were the same. But his face now radiated dignity and power. The two siblings sat in peace, letting the scents and colors and light fill them, until the cool breezes of evening reminded them that they had lives to lead in the community. They walked through the woods back toward home.

As Gwileth and Larso approached their home they looked at each other and in one voice said, "Something's wrong!"

"Yes," said Gwileth. "I feel it in my heart."

Hortishland

They started to run, and as they got closer the sudden weight in their hearts got heavier. They rushed through the kitchen door, only to be met by silence. Something made them afraid to shout. Larso flew up the stairs noiselessly, where he met Darsa.

Chapter Thirty

Darsa looked disheveled and pale. She held her finger to her lips, and as the children approached, she led them into the bedroom where Gerran lay, conscious but in such pain that he hardly saw them. Darsa had put a cold cloth on his forehead, and as she lifted it to replace it with a cooler one, the children saw a large swelling, as if something had hit him very hard.

"It was the hoe," said Darsa. "It happened just as I was going to retrieve it, as I'd promised you, Larso."

Larso collapsed into a chair and held his head in his hands. He groaned. "It's all my fault," he said. "And just at the first time I began to think things were getting better."

"Larso, you mustn't blame yourself. I told you I would get the hoe, so I could blame myself equally," Darsa said. "It just happened. We have no way to know why. Today was so beautiful that he was distracted and wasn't looking where he was going. The hoe was lying on the ground, he stepped on it, and it came up and struck him. That's the way it was."

She knelt down by Larso and hugged him. "He managed to limp home," she said. "I had finished fixing the flowers and was floating in their wonderful scents and colors. As I opened the door to get the hoe, I saw Gerran staggering toward me. I had to help him to get up the stairs, then he told me what happened. His light was so dim I was frightened. It's a little brighter now, but I think we need Drinney. One of you please go for her."

Gwileth was awestruck at the foot of the bed, but Larso was off almost before Darsa made her request. He started running, and as he ran, the terrible truth hit him. I was the one who left the hoe there. I was so eager to go with Gwileth that, without thinking, I threw it aside, telling myself I would put it away when I got back. How could this happen just when my life was beginning to get better?

He felt his three-year-old little griffin roar with frustration and anger. As usual, he was the villain! I can't allow myself to hide under any more chairs, he thought. Then he began to look at the situation more simply and objectively. If this had happened even a week ago I doubt if I could have stood it. But I've become a new person since Philia's meeting, and since being in the woods with Gwileth. It all feels like years ago. The fear that has been with me for so long is now vanquished.

Larso ran between the trees that lined the road, noting how they felt like sentinels, shielding him from anything that might spring out at him in his vulnerable condition. Drinney's little house appeared so quickly that he was surprised he was there already. He ran up the path to the door and knocked.

"Drinney," he called. "Please come. Dad is hurt. It's my fault, and we need you."

When Drinney opened the door, Larso was astonished to find how relieved he felt. He was panting and anxious. He realized what a bulwark Drinney was for Dreamians. She always managed to give her whole attention, her whole heart, to whoever came to her, no matter what the situation.

Drinney looked at Larso carefully and lovingly, evaluating everything about him in seconds, in her clear-sighted way. "You're all right," she said. Then she paced herself to run back to the farm with him, this young man whom she had taught and trained and in whom she delighted.

On the way home Larso explained what had happened, not sparing himself in the telling. Drinney said she had had a premonition and had been ready to go with him when he arrived.

"You are all right, Larso, though you may not think so," she said, as they ran along. "You will do well and I commend you. It hasn't been easy. I know."

Her words bolstered the shaky areas in him and the matters that had been tormenting him. Larso's heart began to expand. He started to feel more complete and whole. He knew that what was to come would test him, but that he was ready.

When they got to the house and up to the bedroom, Darsa and Gwileth were sitting on either side of Gerran, swabbing his swollen brow. Gerran was thrashing from side to side, moaning and trying to hit the air. He was not completely conscious. Drinney took charge, and in her firm and capable manner examined his nasty-looking wound.

"This looks like much more than a hoe could inflict," she said. Then she spoke to Gerran reassuringly. "You have done quite a bit of damage to yourself, Gerran." Gently taking his head in her hands, she started to talk in a strange language. *"Agiri, enu, spahten, arou,"* she intoned. "You will be well again. We will get *alletin* leaves and they will help you, Gerran, but there will be work for you to do. It will require new and different responses from those you have clung to in the past. You may not enjoy making these changes, but they are required for you to regain your health. The whack to your head is not the whole cause of your pain. Anger has filled you with poisons that will have to be removed."

Gerran's light was faint, but as Drinney talked it blinked

on a little stronger. Drinney's flashed very brightly from time to time. She smiled at the others and said, "The testing has begun."

Gerran opened his eyes for an instant, then closed them. Until then he had shown hardly any response to their presence.

Larso and Gwileth looked upon their father's body and saw a person who was helpless and in pain, a person they had never known before, and yet one who had always been there. Gerran had made great efforts to hide the fact that he could be helpless, that it was even a possibility.

Larso's feelings were confused. He knew now he was in charge of every choice he made, free to reject anything imposed on him by others, especially his father. He had slowly established in himself a strong but not combative resistance to manipulations by his father. He had done this to protect his vulnerability and to convey the message that he would no longer be ordered about.

Now the tables had been turned. He was the strong one. It was a heady feeling. At the same time, the "snake," usually coiled and quiescent within him, was saying, "Okay, here's your chance to get even." Larso stopped time to look within. Amazed, he recognized that in spite of all his progress, he still held the weaknesses of humanity, not just the fears, but pride and jealousy and many meannesses that sit ready to take charge whenever they are given the reins. He understood he had the ability to learn from the fact that overcoming one weakness doesn't necessarily mean that all are conquered, and realized that having won one battle did not mean there would be no more conflicts.

Drinney looked at Gerran, then said to Darsa, "He'll sleep for a while now. I have to leave soon, but I'd love a cup of tea. It's wonderful to be with you, even at a time like this, though we'll never catch up with the years we've lost."

Darsa embraced Drinney. "You know we're always together, Drinney, and always will be," she said. "I'm forever grateful to you. We all love you. Now, I think I need a few minutes here alone with Gerran. Then I'll join you downstairs when the tea water has boiled. Both Gwileth and Larso make such splendid tea." Darsa smiled lovingly at her children, and kissed them both as they left the room with Drinney.

In the kitchen, Drinney looked at Larso and Gwileth and said, "I can see this has been a great shock for you. But it is clear to me it has happened for a purpose, so I suggest that you look at it in that light. You will learn from all that takes place. I'll be back tomorrow morning. Until then, there is little to do for your father. I've applied my remedies to take down the swelling. He will sleep and they will work during the night. In the meantime, find alletin leaves that grow at the foot of the mountain. Tomorrow morning we'll make a poultice of them that will be soothing and help to draw out the poisons. You know alletin leaves well. Remember how they healed your hurts and bruises when you were growing up? You were always falling and scraping your knees. Did you ever look for them?"

Gwileth and Larso were making the *ralgo* tea, and listening to Drinney. They gave her a cup, and then sat down at the kitchen table.

"All I know about alletin leaves is that they're green. And somehow I think they're furry," said Gwileth. "Is that right?"

"That's quite right," said Drinney. "What about you, Larso?"

"Well, I have an idea that they're yellow and not very big, and hard to find, but I'm not sure."

Drinney laughed. "If I always put you two together, I think I could find out anything I'd need to know. You're both right, and there's a little more." Drinney sipped her tea with relish. "Alletin leaves are green, furry, small, and hard to find. They are hard to find because they hide. They curl up when anyone comes near, so you have to creep up on them and hope that you can spot them before they curl up. Here's a helpful clue. Their top sides are bluish green and furry, while their undersides are yellow green and smooth. You see yellow when they're hiding, and green when they're open."

"Just how small are they?" asked Gwileth.

"They range from one inch to two, and they are apt to be found in shady places, under trees or between rocks, on hillsides or in the mountains. Be sure to remember to try not to disturb them because they are sensitive.

"We'll do our best," the children said, and got out the baskets, the same ones that had been used for generations by their forebears to harvest plants.

"I wonder why your mother hasn't come down," said Drinney. "I really have to go."

Gwileth ran up the stairs and was back in a second. She was laughing. "Mother's sound asleep in the big chair by father's bed. Father's also asleep. I know she'd have loved to have tea with you, but she must have been exhausted. Your help took all the pressure off her."

"Thanks, Drinney, for everything," the children said. Then they walked outside, Drinney down the lane to Dream, and Gwileth and Larso toward Cranth, the same great mountain where Cloa, their ancestor and the first woman to live on their farm, had made her advent into Hortishland so long ago.

Nobody had had any sleep. They had been too upset to think of time, and when Drinney left, they were too energized. They felt getting alletins for their father was so important that they hardly realized the sun was just rising.

Chapter Thirty-One

*L*et's start calling the farm Gelhanen again," Gwileth said to Larso. "It has such a nice meaning, and I have been feeling the presence of Cloa and Lomay lately, as if they want to share their experiences with us."

"I've had that feeling myself," said Larso. "Wouldn't it be nice if we could see them and talk with them? It sounds as if their lives were very happy from the stories we've heard. *Gelhanen* means something about helping, doesn't it?"

"You're not too far off, Larso. It means 'Serving All,' something else we've forgotten. Shall we hunt for the alletin leaves together or each go a different way? What do you think? Will we find more if we separate?"

They looked up the hill to find out where they wanted to go. A short way up the path they encountered two figures facing them. Larso took Gwileth's hand. The two strangers were an elderly couple, dressed in the clothing of an earlier time.

"Hello," said the children. "Who are you and where have

you come from? We've never seen you before in Dream. Is it possible that you are Cloa and Lomay?"

"You summoned us, didn't you?" Lomay answered. "Why did you want to see us?"

Larso and Gwileth opened their mouths to speak, but nothing came out.

"It's all right," Cloa said. "Of course you're shocked to see us. We're glad to tell you that while we were alive in Dream we were happy. We lived what we knew, the principles and Laws of the Prophecy. Now those on the Outside are suffering for lack of them, as many Dreamians did before the plague."

"We're glad you called on us. We hope you will continue to do so any time when we can be of use to you. Now that you are taking up the challenge of what must be done, we commend you. We urge you to distinguish love from *Love*. You are specially blessed, and with the Dream community, you will help the Outsiders understand what you have learned, and make it part of their lives."

(Since the plague, all Dreamians except Golo and his followers have been trying to attain Eclady, and live more and more in their spirits. This makes the young much more serious than their equivalents Outside. The spirit has no age, only the body ages, only the physical.)

Larso and Gwileth turned to each other in amazement, and when they looked back to respond, no one was there.

"Wow! Did you see what I saw?" asked Larso.

"Wasn't that great?" Gwileth said. "They were so real, and though they lived so long ago they were like the kind of grandparents I'd like to have and spend time with. If we were more aware, I bet we'd see there are many beings with us all the time. We must remember that, even when we don't see them. Can you believe that from those two people and the children that started out with them, came *all* the people of Dream? It was wonderful of them to let us know that they are still with us."

"It was," Larso said. "What do you think they were telling us about love and Love? Isn't love simply love?"

Gwileth looked at her brother quizzically. "Well," she said. "I think they were trying to help us think more deeply, to look at love as not always just love. Pure Love is given freely and asks nothing from anyone. That's the kind they wanted us to recognize as *Love*. Any other kind is not Love. That's what I think."

"Yes, that feels right to me," Larso said. "We'd better start looking for the alletin leaves. Let's go together."

The path up the hill was not steep, and Gwileth trotted happily along, looking under bushes and among the rocks for alletin leaves, but none appeared. The hillside was so beautiful that she sat down to rest for a moment and gaze at her surroundings. It was early morning, cool and fresh, and the sun was shining through the leaves. Bushes lined the path and some had berries. Birds were singing. Gwileth felt so content she forgot about her mission.

Larso kept going, not realizing she wasn't keeping up with him.

Gwileth called out to him, "Hey there, how're you doing?" There was no answer, so she yelled louder. "Larso, where are you?" The birds in the bushes answered with chirping, and the bushes seemed to sigh. I know there's little chance of getting lost here, she thought, and so does Larso, but how could he be beyond earshot? She yelled again, but there was no reply.

Well, I won't starve to death, Gwileth thought, noting the berries on the bushes around her. Suddenly, she realized how hungry she was and, picking a handful from several bushes, she filled her mouth with berries. These are like ambrosia, she thought. Not only were the berries delicious, but they were also wonderfully satisfying. I'll take some of these home to mother, she thought, and started to pick them to fill her basket. At the same time, she looked under each bush in case there were alletins there.

Hortishland

She was so busy that she almost forgot about Larso. Then she remembered and called out again, "Larso, are you there?" But still there was no answer. Far below she saw fields and streams and wooded areas, while ahead the path continued to rise. She started to call again, but heard a voice. "Larso's fine. He has to do his work and you must do yours."

She jerked around at the sound of the voice, and saw that the area on her left had become much brighter.

"Philia," she said. "I feel you are always with me, when I remember, but when I actually *see* you with my eyes, all of me thrills."

Gwileth could see trees and bushes right through Philia, whose "body" was of mists of shimmering iridescence.

To Philia, Gwileth was a lovely young woman whose inner beauty even outshone a beautiful exterior. "I have a message for you and Larso. When Eclady comes for everyone and you find yourselves ready to go to the Outside, you will have what I tell you to rely on. Both of you, with Drinney and the Wise Women, will work with Dreamians to instruct and encourage all the Outsiders you will meet."

"Thank you, Philia. I do know it, though I find it a little frightening," Gwileth said. "I can't find Larso. Do you know where he is? I've been calling him, but he doesn't answer."

Philia clapped her hands, and a path that Gwileth had not noticed before opened up and there was Larso ahead of them with a handful of little green leaves.

Chapter Thirty-Two

*L*arso had been having an adventure of his own. He had started out just a little ahead of Gwileth, but he too had become distracted by the wonderful berry bushes. Hungry, he stuffed himself with berries as he went along, and without realizing it, left Gwileth behind. He noticed that the path was becoming very rocky and full of pebbles that sparkled in unusual colors. He put many of these in his pockets, and soon they became heavy.

He felt ashamed when he realized that he'd been so fascinated he hadn't thought of Gwileth. "Hey, Gwil, can you hear me? Are you finding what I'm finding? Have you seen any alletin plants yet? I haven't seen even one."

At that moment he saw a large clump of yellow leaves a few feet ahead of him. "I wonder if those are alletins," he said, and rushed over to look at them more closely. He realized that there was something invisible in his way. He put out his hand and encountered nothing, but when he tried to get closer he could not take a step. "What's going on?" Wonder and confusion began to assail him. It was then that the alletins began to speak.

"We could see that you were about to spring forward and tear us up, roots and all. You would never have seen us if you were not worthy, so you knew better. We are sacred herbs, as are all gifts of the Earth. You must show your respect and goodwill before you come too close to us." Their little voices were like tinkling bells, yet they had authority.

"Of course I know the laws of care and respect, and I apologize. If you will instruct me I will do whatever you say. I was so glad to think I had found help for my father, that I rushed at you without thinking," said Larso.

At that, the alletin bells began to peal, each on a different note, and Larso was filled with their enchanting sounds. The restraints were relaxed and he could step forward. Following the directions he was given, he began to pick the beautiful leaves, one at a time, careful not to crush the soft, fluffy surfaces. He took only the outside leaves so that the inner leaves could grow and be ready for the next harvest. He put them in his basket and felt as if someone were looking over his shoulder. He looked up and saw Philia smiling at him, radiant and lovely as always.

"Oh, Philia," he said. "I'm glad to see you. Aren't these leaves beautiful? Since you know all that goes on, you probably know of my father's accident. And my part in it, and why I am here."

Philia's smile was full of love and compassion and Larso felt bathed in its unction.

"Don't worry, Larso," she said. "You know now that whatever happens is not an accident, but a message or a test or a lesson from which to learn. The accident disordered your life, but you will find it has enlarged it as well. It will give you new challenges that will help you grow. It is a gift that will strengthen your spirit, and give you the ability to handle future adventures. It was necessary for your father, too. Don't ever go with your initial reactions. Be aware, and *choose* a conscious, caring path for Outsiders to follow. They are starving for such insights. Your mission is to feed them."

Larso looked at Philia in bewilderment.

"Don't worry, Larso. I'm just letting you know what will someday take place. Listen quietly and you will know all you need to know in plenty of time. If you could only realize it, Larso, things often fall into place for you. But you are always so busy trying to make them work out the way you think they 'should,' and so busy criticizing whatever doesn't work your way, that you're oblivious to how perfect each moment of your life is. Someday you will realize this. Still, look. Do you see anything new around you now?"

"Holy daw! Where did they all come from?" said Larso, astounded. "They weren't here just a second ago."

There were alletins everywhere, no longer yellow or closed. Their leaves were every shade of green, covered with the softest, fluffiest fur. "Now that you have learned how to pick them, they trust you. They know they don't have to hide any longer, so pick your basket full," said Philia. "They dry beautifully, and will be useful fresh or dried. Savor this moment, for it may also be that you never return to this sacred area. If you get too many alletins, I'm sure Jom would love to have some for his store."

By this time, Gwileth had come up the path, admiring and picking up the sparkling pebbles she saw, just as Larso had.

Larso looked at Gwileth with her basket full of berries, and realized that he had forgotten everything except his mission to collect alletins. "I'm sorry, Gwil," he said. "I got ahead of you, and the alletins were so interesting that I forgot you. Please forgive me. But aren't they wonderful?"

Gwileth looked at the carpet of greens spread out around them. She'd arrived so quietly that she hadn't disturbed the alletins. She heard their welcoming bells pealing lightly and realized how subtle they were: They only allowed their sounds to be heard when a person stopped to listen intently.

"I had no idea how lovely they'd be," she exclaimed.

Larso showed Gwileth how he picked the leaves, and with great care they filled his basket.

When they had all they could take, Larso went back to the first alletin, the one that had taught him the art of reverencing the plant world. He spoke to it from a deep place within himself. "I thank you and all of your family for your generosity, and for the healing properties you share." The alletins in reply became more colorful and melodic, and opened and closed in unison.

Philia was watching them say good-bye to the alletins. "Now that I have you alone together, I want to tell you the message. I have been saving this for you. It will help you whenever you need to act wisely and quickly, especially when you are with those on the Outside."

There was a large patch of thick, soft moss under a cheeb tree nearby, and the two young people sat on it together, eager to hear what Philia had to tell them.

Gwileth asked, "When will that be, Philia? I don't feel like meeting anyone new right now. I know I have a lot more to learn before I can act wisely, especially with strangers who have a lot of troubles."

Philia smiled, and joined them on the soft moss. "Don't worry, Gwileth," she said. "You will not be called upon until you are ready. I think it will help you both when you will need it, to hear this now.

"The people of Hortishland have a sacred charge to bring the Outside world into a realization that will save it from its path, which is rushing them to disaster. Your forebears came from the Outside, and that is why you have the same temptations and weaknesses that they have.

"You and Hortishans everywhere must understand the principles, and you must also live them until you know no other way to live. Then, when Eclady comes to every one of you and you find yourselves among Outsiders who will believe that you are one of them, you will never need to preach. Your living example will teach them all they will need. That is why Hortishans who deteriorated to the level of Outsiders paid the price of the plague. It's why the Wise Women have become so wise. They spent many years before the plague learning the meaning of the Prophecy. They each suffered in different ways, and thus matured, until wisdom became their mainstay and saved their lives.

"Thanks to our monthly meetings, here and in every Hortishland, the concepts of how to travel on the upward path are becoming clearer. The path to maturity is a spiral staircase that is difficult to climb. It leads to a room of exquisite proportions. There, understanding supersedes being informed, cleverness is replaced with wisdom, and respect and compassion are supreme.

"For those who have not climbed the spiral staircase, like many Outsiders, their sense of themselves is apt to be higher than their sense of others. Their greatest failure is that they see their fellow beings as other than themselves.

"Outsiders, when you are among them, will learn these things from you simply by osmosis. People, even the most sophisticated, actually *are* animals and do all the things that animals do. Just having that realization would change the egocentric climate that pervades much of the Outside population, yet almost all deny their animal selves, and are totally unconscious that they have the capacity to become great beings that could be much more than they imagine is possible.

"No human being is lesser or greater than any other."

Philia became more like a mist than like anything solid and physical. Gwileth said, "Philia, don't leave us. We can hardly see you."

Larso said, "I'm confused. You're telling us what we will show to Outsiders whom we've never seen. From what I've heard, they wouldn't pay attention if I told them anything. How is this all going to come about?"

"It's all right." Philia's form became brighter, and they felt a loving warmth enfold them. "You are always being guided at each moment. If you are aware, you will have no doubts about what you will do or say. You must also know that, in the spirit, time does not exist.

"I am going now."

Larso and Gwileth saw that a new downward path had appeared on the hill, and they started down it, carrying their baskets. Almost immediately, it seemed, they were back at the farm.

Chapter Thirty-Three

The farm had always seemed large and impressive to the children, but as they approached it this time, it looked smaller, as if it had shrunk since they were last home.

Gwileth pulled on Larso's sleeve to slow him down. "Everything is changing so fast," she said. "Does the farm look smaller to you?"

"It certainly does," said Larso. "But I have a feeling that it's we who are making the changes. Each time I see Philia, something important seems to shift in me and I see everything differently."

"That seems right to me," said Gwileth.

She stopped and gave Larso a penetrating look. "I know dealing with the situation at home is not easy for you, but you are becoming more and more clear about who you are and what matters to you. You know I'll be behind you, no matter what, and Mother will be, too."

"I do know, Gwil," said Larso. "Whatever happens, we're together and will be as long as we can."

As they approached the house, the aroma of soup filled the air, and they said in unison, "calbad soup," and burst out laughing.

Darsa had awakened to find the house silent and Gerran still in a deep sleep. The cloth on his forehead and the lingering scent of herbs reminded her that Drinney had been there. She jumped up, thinking that her dear friend and the children might still be waiting for her with the ralgo tea, but the kitchen was deserted. The kettle was simmering and a clean cup and saucer were on the table. She realized that she had slept through the night and it was morning. Darsa's heart filled with gratitude, and then she remembered that Drinney had mentioned alletin leaves. A note on the table told her that her friend could not wait, and had sent Larso and Gwileth after the healing herbs.

They hadn't had a calbad for a while and there was a large one in the vegetable bed ready for picking. She checked to make sure that Gerran had not awakened, then went to the garden, the sanctuary that had helped her to keep her sanity so many times. Once again she felt its healing embrace. Vegetables and flowers seemed to greet her, and as she planned what she'd put in the soup, she thanked the earth, the rain, the air, and the sun for their contributions to her health, for the size and beauty of the flowers and vegetables. She sang while she filled her basket.

It was a clear day and her spirits were high as she filled the big pot with the garden produce. The stove was at the right temperature for simmering, so she put the pot on and sat down to rest. She sipped her ralgo tea, feeling great satisfaction, as if she had accomplished something special.

Then she had a creepy feeling that someone was with her. Before she could think, a figure lunged at her, seemingly from out of nowhere, brandishing a small, menacing instrument. She drew back in shock, not having time to fear, and said, "Who are you?"

It was Golo. She hadn't seen him for years, but everyone in Dream knew Golo because of his placyl. "Why are you here, Golo? What do you want?"

On some people, she had seen the light on their heads turn red when they were disturbed. She had seen it happen when her children had been angry and when Gerran had vented his angry feelings. But Golo's light had an extra redness she had never seen. She knew she was in danger.

"Golo," Darsa said, trying not to sound frightened. "What is that in your hand and what are you trying to do?"

Golo's eyes were wild with rage. He was out of control. He stared at her and yelled, "She left me, and you're still here. Why? Why? Why? Morca took care of the children, and made the meals, and kept the house neat and quiet so I could do my inventing. Now she's gone! I'm going to *drent* you with my new invention, my *sark,* and take you home with me. You'll do whatever I want done. When I put this on your light, you will be in my power."

Darsa tried to get up, but Golo held her down with one hand, as he wielded the sark over her head. At that moment Larso and Gwileth came into the kitchen chatting and laughing. Gwileth saw that Golo was dangerous. She saw his ugly light, his threatening expression, and then the shiny thing in his hand. She dropped her basket, and streaking across the room, lunged for the instrument in time to prevent its contact with Darsa's light.

For his part, Golo saw a dragon flash and leap at him, yet he was also aware of a lovely young girl hitting the sark with such force that he nearly dropped it.

Darsa jumped up, and Golo tried to run, but Larso grabbed him and wrestled the weapon from his hand. "All right, Golo. What is this thing? What were you trying to do with it to our mother?"

Darsa was shaken by the events, then she saw that Larso had Golo in hand and began to feel safer.

"Gwileth," she said, "you were wonderful, so aware and so quick. Thank you, love."

To Larso, holding Golo in his strong grasp, she said, "You are becoming the one I have always believed you would be. Do be careful, son, Golo is not to be trusted. His mind is out of control. Look at the color of his light."

"I need something to bind him with," Larso said. "Maybe we can talk with him and find out what he's up to."

Gwileth brought him the kitchen tablecloth, and Larso used it to tie Golo securely to a chair.

Larso was shaking, but he wanted so badly to be in charge of the situation that he sat down in front of Golo, and tried to sound strong. "Now," he said, "what's going on, and why are you here?"

Golo started to spit at Larso, so Larso found a cloth napkin and tied it over Golo's mouth. Golo made noises, but had to finally simmer down. Larso tried to bring his own feelings under control and figure out the frightening situation. "Will you tell us what you were doing to Mother, and what this thing we took away from you is?"

Just then a loud groan sounded from above, and the three nearly knocked one another over as they scrambled to climb the stairs.

"We forgot Gerran. How amazing!" They were aghast at how they had forgotten Gerran. When they got to his room he was sitting up, holding his head in his hands.

"I feel terrible. Where have you all been? I'm thirsty." His words came tumbling out, growling and accusatory.

Larso was surprised to find he felt relieved rather than intimidated. His father's usual behavior, unpleasant as it was, was so familiar and predictable that it had lost its ability to strike terror in his heart. Also, he believed now that his strength was enough to do whatever was needed, without fear or anger toward his now helpless father.

Gerran tried to get up. He put one foot over the side of the bed, and then the other, but when he tried to stand he fell back, dizzy and disoriented. One of his knees was swollen and distorted.

Darsa said, "Gerran, what's the matter with your knee?" But Gerran pulled it back, hid it under the covers, and didn't answer. "It looks as if you will have to stay in bed for a few days," Darsa continued. She was trembling. Too much was going on. She was very glad to have Larso and Gwileth with her. Darsa collapsed into a chair, and Larso said, "Mother, what can we do?"

"Gwileth, please get some new cloths and soak them in pingar oil for Gerran's head. And you, Larso, just do whatever you think will help. Drinney will be here again in the morning, Gerran, and will tell us how you are doing. So rest as well as you can, and know that we will do whatever is possible to help you recover."

Gerran tried to get up, only to fall back again. His face flushed crimson, and he shouted, "Get out of here, all of you! I will take care of myself! And, what do you mean Drinney is coming here? Didn't I forbid you to have her ever come here again?" He choked and fell back on the pillows exhausted. He was out of his head, ranting and raving, not knowing what he was saying. Fear of his helplessness took over. He was unaware of what had happened downstairs.

Gwileth went to her father, thinking she might calm him, but he yelled at her. "You keep out of this, too! Get out of here!" They knew it was no use to tell him about Golo.

Larso realized that Gerran was unable to get out of bed, and he must need a "pot." Larso got a clay vase and said, "If you use this, Father, you'll feel better."

Gerran was getting a terrible headache, and was becoming almost apoplectic with fury. He tried to shout, but he had no power left. "Get out," he mumbled, and accepted his son's homemade chamber pot, while Darsa and Gwileth went into the hall to discuss the situation.

"Now," Darsa said, returning to the room, "I need Larso to do some things for me downstairs. Gwileth has agreed to stay with you for a while. See if you can get some sleep. We'll bring you a bowl of calbad soup when it is ready."

The room had become filled with the delicious aroma of soup. She felt Gerran's forehead, but he pulled away and growled at her. She decided not to mention Drinney again until she was actually there. Then she and Larso, after taking the vase from his father, went down to the kitchen to figure out what to do with Golo.

Golo was securely trussed. His eyes were blazing, but his light had become the red of normal anger. He was no longer dangerous.

"Father is very ill," Larso said. "We don't want him upset, so if you can talk quietly, I will take this cloth off your mouth. Just shake your head, yes or no."

Golo glared, so Darsa ladled the calbad soup into two wooden bowls. Larso took them to Gwileth and Gerran, and then joined Darsa at the table. The soup was hot and satisfying and they relished it with the dark bread Darsa had made from kloff flour the day before.

Golo sat watching them, becoming more aware of how hungry he was, but stubbornly not wanting to admit it. Larso glanced at him from time to time and noticed his light kept changing, from anger to what he supposed was the color of hunger. (The Hortish people's lights were magical. Any feeling could be discerned by the practiced eye of any other Hortishan. It helped them to get along with each other.) Larso asked Golo again if he would speak quietly. Golo finally nodded his head in assent. Larso removed the napkin gag. Still glowering, Golo opened and closed his mouth several times, then finally spoke.

"One day when I was walking I found a rock in the foothills," he said. "It drew me to it. I couldn't resist its magnetism. It was silvery and shiny, and had a pinkish glow. It was like nothing I'd ever seen before."

Golo shifted in his chair and looked suspiciously at Larso and Darsa. They said nothing, and he continued. "A small piece of it came off in my hand, so I took it home to find out more about it. I carved what you see there, my first sark, from it. While I carved it, I felt many feelings that were new to me. They were frightening. I hid it from Brul and Sheil, and stayed in my workroom, where no one else is allowed. One night when the boys were asleep I went into their room and put the sark on Brul's light. He got out of bed and became like a docile pet trog. He had always been independent, but now he followed me around, eager to do anything I wanted. I was terrified. What had I done to my son? Sheil was horrified, too. He ran out of the house into the field where they say there's a mound, though I've yet to see it. I don't know what this piece of rock can do, but I suspect many things more than I imagine. I do know that it is very powerful."

He was sitting on the edge of his chair, and his light was shining brightly and clearly.

Golo has the power to be a good man, Darsa thought. Given a chance, he might even help with our mission to save Outsiders. We've maligned him, have never let him show us more than his angry side.

Golo continued. "Sheil didn't come back that night. When Brul was asleep, I got out the sark again. I don't know whether you noticed, but one end has a pinkish cast to it, while the other is greenish. I had put the pink end to his head the first time, so this time I tried the green, hoping he would return to normal.

"When I reversed the sark, he jumped up even quicker than before, took one look at me, and stormed out of the house, just as Sheil had done. That's when I got the idea to subdue you, Darsa. My sons are very little help to me, though I admit they're hardly any trouble to me, either. They're busy outside all the time. I don't know what they're doing. They are always disappearing into the field. I'm still angry with Morca for leaving me. Don't tell me she couldn't help it. I know it, but that just makes me even angrier."

Golo's light began to turn red again and Larso said, "Golo, trying to take our mother wasn't the answer for you. It would have been very bad for us, too. Your inventing is important to Hortishans, but it's clear that you need help. There are other ways to get it. Why don't you ask around town? I'm sure there are people who would be glad to give you what you need. Even cook for you. As a matter of fact, I've always been interested in inventions, too, and would like to know more about yours. Would you let me learn from you?"

Darsa had recovered from the shock of Golo's attack and began to look at him with the eyes of her inner self. I must have compassion for this man, she thought. That is one of the Laws. "If you'd like to come by here from time to time, we'll be glad to have you join us for a meal," she said. "When Gerran is feeling better it would be a help for him to have you to talk with. If you have the time, he has problems in the orchard. I'm sure he'd discuss them with you."

What am I saying, Darsa thought. Just a short time ago I didn't want them near each other.

Golo was nonplussed. "Do you mean that?" He was embarrassed.

Darsa and Larso were almost as shocked with her magnanimity as Golo was embarrassed. Somehow they knew that what they were saying was right and necessary.

"Yes," they said with one voice, "we mean it."

Darsa stood up then, and said, "Golo, you have had a hard time. That doesn't have to continue. We and the community need you for all sorts of things. Everyone who has a placyl loves it, and most Dreamians use many of your gadgets. They will be glad to have new inventions. So why don't you go home now, and come back whenever you like."

Larso untied Golo and gave him a bowl of soup, which he ate ravenously. Then he went for the sark. "No, Golo," Larso said, stepping in between. "We'll keep it here. It's yours, and we will give it back at a better time, but as a sign of good faith, leave it here for a while. If you like, we'll experiment with it together, soon."

Golo was stunned. What was happening? He had threatened and been nasty to Darsa and Larso, and they had not retaliated. All sorts of things were changing. His sons no longer fought him as they once had. He'd attributed that to their growing up. He suddenly thought: they had changed the most since they'd been going to those meetings, which they had been urging him to attend.

He thought about his small band of cronies who were angry with everything and everybody. They'd all had losses from the plague, and they blamed all their problems on this, but never seemed able to overcome them. Their company was losing its appeal for him. They seemed childish, less companionable. Golo was confused as he staggered out of the house.

Darsa and Larso looked at each other triumphantly. "It works," they said. "Philia will be pleased."

A voice in the air said, "Yes, I am."

Mother and son hugged, then went upstairs to see how Gwileth and Gerran were faring. They were amused to find Gwileth asleep in the big chair, the same chair that had cradled Darsa a short time ago. Gerran had resigned himself to sleep, and it was beginning to get dark. They realized, for the first time, what a full day it had been. Tomorrow Drinney would come again to see Gerran. She would tell them what to expect, how long she thought he would have to stay in bed, and how soon he would be able to work in the orchard again. Gwileth stirred in the chair, and without waking her, Darsa and Larso led her to her room, then retired themselves.

As they parted for the night, Larso asked Darsa, "Do you suppose that the sark is made from the Rock of Knowing?"

"If it is," said Darsa, "we must get Golo to show the community where the Rock is right away. Finding that Rock has been one of Philia's most important assignments for us. It is crucial for all Hortishlands. It wasn't even a certainty that it would be found here. If it actually is the Rock of Knowing, isn't it ironic that Golo was the one to discover it?"

Chapter Thirty-Four

That night it rained heavily, and in the morning the sun shone on a glistening, well-scrubbed world. Drinney arrived with a basket of *rinter* berries. Gwileth made muffins with them and told Drinney the events of the day before, between bites of muffin and sips of tea.

Drinney was excited about the sark. She held it and closed her eyes. Vibrations went from it up her arm, and feeling its power, she said, "It must be a piece of the Rock of Knowing. It is like nothing I know. We'll have to let the community know about it and have Golo show us where the Rock is as soon as possible.

"How exciting! You and Larso were wonderful with Golo. You gave him a chance to see himself as not being rejected. You acted from your hearts rather than from judgment," she said, turning to Darsa. "We're all learning what's important from Philia, and you put it into action very well. I can't wait to find out what *he* learned next time you see him. But I guess we better go look at the patient now."

"Dad is going to be very disagreeable," Larso warned her.

"He still thinks he can make us jump by yelling at us. He doesn't realize that he needs us and can't do much without us. So be prepared."

"He's done something to his knee," Gwileth said, "that we didn't know about yesterday. It looks broken or dislocated. The bump on his head doesn't look like it's only from a hoe, either."

Drinney smiled. "It looked like that to me, too," she said.

"We'll be with you whatever he does," Larso said. "So he'll have to let you help him."

"I'll manage," Drinney assured them. "I've become used to people who, when they feel helpless, let off their fear and anger at me. They soon relent. I've known Gerran long enough to know he is not as tough as he pretends to be. So I'm not worried."

Darsa went upstairs to see if Gerran had wakened, then called down to them several minutes later to come up. When Drinney walked into the room, Gerran refused to look at her, acting as if he thought not seeing her would prevent her from being present. Drinney paid no attention. "How are you feeling?" she asked. He didn't answer. "You look much better than yesterday," she continued, and examined his head. "Hmm, healing nicely," she said.

"You weren't here yesterday, and I don't want you here now." Gerran could not restrain himself any longer "Go away!"

"Let's take a look at your knee," Drinney said, pulling the covers aside.

Gerran pulled them back again. "I told you to go away," he snapped. "Didn't you hear me?"

Drinney ignored him, and pulled the covers back again. His foot was turned to the side and his knee looked swollen and badly twisted. "Oh," she exclaimed. "I don't like the look of this. I'll need everyone's help, yours too, Gerran."

"Go away, all of you," Gerran repeated, and tried to pull

the covers up again. Drinney took the others aside and instructed them.

"Fortunately I brought some *gria* oil with me," she said. "It will deaden the pain when we straighten his knee, but putting it on may hurt a little, so I'm counting on you to cooperate," she added for Gerran's benefit.

Drinney went back to the bed and gently applied the oil to the injured knee. Gerran tried to pull his leg away, but that hurt more than Drinney's ministrations. He lay back and gave up. Drinney continued rubbing in the oil until she could move his foot back and forth without it hurting him.

"Now," she said, "since Larso is the strongest I will need him to hold Gerran's foot firmly while I straighten the knee. Is there any story you can tell to your father, Gwileth?"

"As a matter of fact," said Gwileth, "there's the one you told us in school, 'The Vanishing Pallas.' That might be good."

"Oh, I remember that," said Larso. "Good choice, Gwil."

"All right," said Drinney. "Darsa, could you get some tea for all of us, and a little palla wine for Gerran? It will help him when we're finished."

Gerran was lying back, defeated. He knew there was nothing he could do, that nobody would join him in arguing.

"Gerran, this will hurt, but just for a moment," Drinney said. "If I don't do it, it will hurt a great deal more. Relax as well as you can, will you?" Gerran lowered his head slightly in assent.

"Now, Larso, hold your father's foot." Drinney took the injured knee in both hands, and when Larso said he was ready, pulled and straightened it with a jerk. There was a cracking sound from the knee and a roar from Gerran. Drinney felt the knee and said, "Sorry, Gerran. I know it was a big shock, but your knee will heal straight and be fine now. You would never have been able to walk again if I hadn't done that. Ah, here comes Darsa with some wine for you."

As he sipped his wine, Drinney looked Gerran in the eye

and said, "Okay, Gerran, tell us what happened. It wasn't the hoe, was it?"

Gerran tried not to meet her gaze, but in halting tones he admitted that before he stepped on the hoe, he had not been watching what he was doing. When he had pruned a big palla branch, it had fallen on his foot. This had so annoyed him that he kicked the branch and twisted his knee. Then he hit his head hard on another large limb. When he stepped on the hoe, it only damaged his forehead some more. He only mentioned the hoe because he wanted to blame his negligence on something else.

What an admission for Father, who usually doesn't admit anything, thought Larso. A surge of relief filled him, and he felt power he had never known before.

"You were so quick, Drinney. I didn't even begin my story," Gwileth said.

"That's all right, Gwileth," Drinney said, and gave Larso a knowing look that completed his emancipation.

"It took your mind off what was being done, Gwileth, and since your father will not be going far for a while, you will have many more opportunities to tell your story to him. Let's all have tea, now, and encourage your father to get well."

Gerran drank the wine eagerly, and the others felt calmer as they drank their tea. Then Drinney said, "I need you all to participate in the healing. Gwileth and Larso, take one of your father's hands. Your mother and I will take each other's and yours. We will now go within ourselves, and I hope you will too, Gerran, to unite our healing powers and direct them where they are most needed."

The room darkened perceptibly, and humming sounds seemed to come from Gerran's body while the little group concentrated. Gerran's light, which had weakened, grew stronger, and Drinney made humming sounds that enhanced those coming from Gerran. All felt filled with a wonderful peace, and the room brightened.

Drinney said to Gwileth, "There is something that I need

from you. Do you know if there are any dry pieces of elpalm wood in the shed?"

Gwileth looked at Drinney with surprise, "How strange. I made a pile of short sticks of elpalm just last week. I didn't know why, but I saw the ax and there was a log and I *knew* I was to chop it into thin sticks."

"They're just what I need," Drinney said. "And, Darsa, if you or Larso know where there is something to bind the sticks with to keep Gerran's knee in position, please get it."

Gwileth came back almost immediately with the sticks, and soon Darsa came with a basin of what looked like mud. "Like Gwileth, I've been keeping this and kneading it, to make it light and porous, but I've had no idea what I'd use it for."

"You're beginning to catch on," Drinney said with a laugh. "I don't have to tell you, do I, that when you are in touch with your inner knowing you don't have to think about the whys of things at all. You do what needs doing when it arises. Where did you get that *clail*, Darsa?"

"So, that's what it is," said Darsa. "I wondered. I found it in the garden, and was drawn to it, so I brought some in."

Larso came in while Darsa was talking. "Look what I've got," he said. "I brought this home with me from my time in the woods with Gwileth. One of the Earth spirits gave it to me." He held up a spider web, beautiful as spider webs are, but stronger, not as sticky, and very stretchy. "I was wondering what I would do with this."

"Now we have everything we need." Drinney announced. She put handfuls of clail on Gerran's leg, embedded the elpalm sticks in it to strengthen it, and then bound the cast with the spider's web. "With this on your knee, the heat from your body will dry it almost instantly, and your knee will be protected from bumps or turning. You must not try to stand on it for a few days though, and then only for a short time." Drinney turned and smiled at Gerran. "Good-bye. There are others waiting for me, so I must go."

Hortishland

Gerran was not ready to thank her, but he knew Drinney had saved his knee. He put his hand out and said good-bye.

Darsa and the children went downstairs with Drinney and each told her how grateful they were for helping heal Gerran.

Chapter Thirty-Five

*G*olo did not sleep well after his experience at the farm. A battle was raging within him. In his dreams there were hoards of feisty little men, all fighting each other. Some were blue and their opponents were red. Some were fat while others were thin. All night long they argued violently, and occasionally blows were exchanged. Sometimes Golo found himself deep in the fray, but more often, he was observing from the sidelines, wringing his hands and beseeching the combatants to stop fighting and listen to one another.

The fighting mostly confined itself to recriminations. Some were shouting, "You're always complaining. Why don't you help me when I want you to?" Others bellowed, "Everyone in Dream is against us, and they say nasty things about us at their meetings. Let's get them." Others bragged, "We're the most important ones here, but no one appreciates us, so why should we do anything to help them." The fighting went on and on.

When Golo was part of the skirmishes he felt protected

and safe, but when he was standing on the edge of the pit where they were fighting, he felt if they did not stop what, to him, had become craziness, the bottom of the pit would give way and they would all sink into a much deeper pit that had no escape. He could see how wrong their reasoning was. Golo knew they were making up stories to keep their anger fueled, without even trying to verify their accusations.

It was also clear in his dream that after the afternoon's experience at the Bavres farm, those they were vilifying were people they had never made any effort to get to know. It was their own discontent they were blaming on everyone else, just as he had blamed his loneliness and anger on Morca. Golo realized that he had felt, unconsciously, that she was his best bet to attack since she couldn't defend herself. He began to see that wasn't fair. So he tossed and turned all night, and when he could stay in bed no longer, Golo got up.

He looked outside, and saw the sun shedding its first rays on every drop of dew, on every stalk and stem in Byphon's field. The light turned the field into a glistening fairyland, and there, as big as a house, was the mound, or bump, as the boys called it, in the middle of his view. He looked at it, looked away, and then back at it again, but it didn't go away.

He was surprised to feel a yearning to go closer to it, but at the same time he was gripped by fear. Why hadn't he seen this before? Had it been there when Brul and Sheil had talked about it? What was it? Nonstop questions raced through his mind. Maybe it would be better to pretend he still couldn't see it; then his life could go on as it had, but did he want that? It hadn't been such a happy life.

He went toward the strange object. It was huge and looked solid. As he approached it, one of his group, a man called Darg with whom he had often spent time complaining about life, walked across the field toward him. Golo was about to say good morning, when he realized his friend didn't see him at all. He kept walking, right through the mound as if it didn't exist, then continued and passed within three inches of Golo. "This is too much," Golo said out loud in shock.

When he was able to move again, he started toward the mound, eager and reluctant. His heart was pounding, fear gripped him, and he felt dizzy.

There were no signs of his boys, so Golo guessed there was an entrance and that they were already inside, but looking at the mound, he didn't see any doors or windows. Its walls were of a material that fascinated the inventor in him. They had no seams or edges, and were not made of clay nor of any wood that he knew; the walls felt warm and silken, the most beautiful color he had ever seen, a mixture of all colors. He heard voices calling, wings fluttering, and then he saw the entrance. "What a pair of doors!" he said to himself.

The doors were closed. They looked like wings, crossed in self-protection. Above them was an exquisite head made of stone, similar to the rock he had found in the hills and out of which he had made the sark. Golo stared at it in disbelief. Then its eyes opened and looked into his. He wanted desperately to run, but found himself unable to move a muscle. Then the head spoke: "Welcome, Golo."

Looking into those magnificent eyes, Golo felt welcome for the first time in his life. Tears rose in his eyes, and he collapsed in a heap. "This can't be real," he said.

"It is real," said the head. "My name is Ariel, and I'm a close friend of Byphon. What you are now seeing is as real as anything you have ever seen. You may enter."

As Ariel spoke, the wing doors began to move apart, and Golo was once again filled with fear. What would he find inside?

Chapter Thirty-Six

*G*olo stood before the mound in awe; the opening looked like the entrance to a chasm. He took a step reluctantly, and felt as if a magnet were pulling him forward. He had always thought he was in control, but now he knew he controlled nothing. He shivered as he was drawn in, but just as his fear began to overwhelm him, the darkness turned to light.

Golo shook his head in disbelief, but thought, "It's all been so strange so far, why couldn't it be this way, too?"

The light was so bright at first he could see nothing. It bathed him like butterfly wings, soft and soothing, all over him. Then he began to see. He was no longer on his feet, but sitting in midair in a meditative position. Facing him in midair were Sheil and Brul, their faces suffused with delight. "Welcome, Father," they said. "We have been hoping and waiting for this moment for a long time."

Golo kept saying, to no one in particular, "This can't be real. I must be dreaming." But it was real. He looked at his two sons, fine, capable young men. He felt humbled in their presence. "I have not been a good father to you, and yet you welcome me. Thank you." Tears filled his eyes.

Golo saw that the mound's ceiling was lit by stars, giving it the look of a night sky. A purple circle was in the center of it, and enchanting music filled the three of them.

A voice that came from everywhere at once said, "Golo. It is a great pleasure to have you here. You have learned much in a very short time. The fog that has kept you blind for so long has lifted. You are ready to move ahead, to join your sons and the Dream community. Every Dreamian is needed to bring success to the efforts to teach the Outsiders what they need to survive."

"Byphon, that sounds like you—is it?" Golo asked. "This is all so new to me. I'm overcome." Golo felt filled with strength and energy. "I am very glad to be here," he said simply.

"Yes, you're right. I am the Byphon you once knew as a cladloc, but I am no longer the same. I have made many images of myself and can be in all Hortishlands at once. I have made mounds similar to this in each Hortishland. I have instructed all the residents who are attaining Eclady to gather in them. Then I can speak to every one of them at once.

"These mounds are magical structures. They were built to be one of the rewards of Eclady. Until you, Golo, became aware of yourself as an integral part of this community and were filled with goodwill, you could not see this mound. The same was true for others. The transition did not take place in a moment. It began for you when Darsa and her children were kind to you. You have been sorting your ideas and feelings ever since. Your life will be full and active now, happier than you ever imagined. You will have a large part to play in the completion of Dream's work. You are 'cream' that has been unable to rise because of your belief that you were a victim. Many Outsiders are disabled by this same misperception. Now you can rise to the top.

You will be a model for Outsiders. I leave you and your boys to choose the course you will take, and I wish you well."

The stars above them danced and flashed while Golo and his sons descended gently to the grassy spot where Sheil and Brul had first learned to sit together. Golo looked at his sons. He felt so many emotions that he could not speak. Gratitude won. "Thank you both again for bearing with me," Golo said. "I realize I have been angry and sorry for myself for so long, I have not seen or heard anyone else, even you, my children. You have taken the brunt of it many times, even physically. Now I want to start a new life and contribute to your welfare and to the community. I want to do anything I can to help, anywhere I am able.

"I thought I loved your mother, but I'm beginning to realize that what I thought was love was a combination of lust and a desire to own her, and to have her serve me. Poor Morca. I have been angry, blaming her all these years, while neglecting you and feeling deserted myself. I brought about my own abandonment. I was self-centered and unpleasant to everyone. I was trapped in self-pity, unaware of the feelings and needs of others. But now I feel free to see all I missed. Now I can care. It's wonderful.

"I haven't known anything or anyone, except for my three angry old friends and cronies, for a long time. We've spent years venting our rage, avoiding anyone who might disagree with us. Poor men! Someday I hope I can show them what I have found."

"That's great, Dad," both boys assured him. "What has been is all over now. What do you think, Dad? Could this be your Eclady?'

"We have something to tell you now that may interest you, Dad," Sheil said. "We've been talking with the Wise Women. Do you remember your Aunt Fado? She's little and her voice is like a bird's high chirps, and she's delightful."

"Yes, I think I remember slightly an aunt who used to play

with me when I was a child. She was little, like I was then, and fun. I liked her a lot."

"Well, the Wise Women have agreed to tell anybody what they have learned about the Outside," said Brul. "They have made contact telepathically with Jad Bavres, who left Dream long ago when he was a boy. He has been living in a place called New York City. The Wise Women say they are learning a lot about his experiences, and about what he has learned.

"We are inviting all of Dream to come next week to get to know each other better. Jom is sure to be there. It will be great to acquaint our friends with our 'new' father. We'll meet inside the mound. It has the ability to become smaller or larger to fit the needs of any group. It should be a marvelous evening."

While Brul spoke, the domed ceiling had become deep green. Pointing to the center of it, he said, "The green dome is always soothing and healing to anyone beneath it. When there are expanding purple circles in the middle, we know that Byphon is here, to listen or communicate with us. The rest of the time, scenes, mostly of nature, will glide across it and keep our spirits buoyed. You see why we spend so much time here?"

Sheil said, "Dad, I know this is pretty amazing for you, but what do you see is needed now?"

As if another voice were speaking from within him, Golo found himself answering. "There is a rock I came upon a short time ago. Just by chance, or so it seemed. It was out in the hills—shiny, silvery, with a pinkish glow. It drew me to it, and I brought a piece of it home to study. You didn't realize it at the time, Sheil, but when Brul started to act like a pet trog, it was because I was experimenting on him with the rock. It also returned him to normal. Larso has that piece now because I used it wrongly, trying to get Darsa under its spell. But you see, I'm convinced I must find that rock again and learn its uses."

This excited Sheil and Brul. "It's got to be the Rock of Knowing," said Sheil. "We were told that a piece of the original Rock of Knowing has been placed in every Hortishland. It was too complicated to have it in only one place. You must have found ours, the one for this Hortishland. Maybe ours is the original one that Trera carved."

Brul paced back and forth, "It's amazing. So much is happening at once. You don't know this, Father, because you have never met Philia. But finding our Rock of Knowing is what's needed for the success of the mission of all Hortishlands. *Where* did you find it?"

"That's what's so strange," Golo confessed. "It's as if my mind were a slate that had all the information on it that anyone needs to find it. Then someone wiped it clean. There is not even a hint of where it is. All I can remember is that I started out into the hills from the school, and I don't think I climbed very high. The rock isn't big, but it has great power. I could *feel* it even before I saw it. The sark has powers that I fear, yet I want to understand them."

"My guess is that it was decided long ago who will find the Rock of Knowing and that it won't be long until it happens," said Brul. "You have not been prepared for this, but whoever has will be helped. Philia has been telling us this for months. But I think all of Hortishland will benefit from the inventions you will make with the Rock of Knowing."

Chapter Thirty-Seven

"The word 'community' brings many images to mind," said Gara, the Wise Woman who was Drinney's cousin, as she stood by the counter in Jom's store. She was talking to whoever wanted to listen, as she picked up her provisions. Other Dreamians were there for the same purpose, so it was a busy day at Jom's. Gara spoke in her lovely, melodic voice. All who heard her felt caressed by its soothing tones as she asked them, "Would you like to hear what we've learned about the Outside world?" The response was immediate and affirmative, and a hush ensued.

"In the Outside world, there are scattered communities in which a spirit of cooperation and mutual concern is encouraged," Gara said. "These are just small pockets of people compared to the population of the Earth. Those there make a valiant effort to live in harmony with nature and each other. They do not exclude anyone, no matter how different.

"They strive to be productive, to waste nothing, to have

deeper, spiritually focused lives. It is often not easy, but some manage well. Most of these groups are confined to themselves. They do not realize that, if they are to survive, they must recognize that humanity is *one* humanity, *one* community.

"This is one of the messages that Hortishans will have to spread when their time comes. It's the lesson they are beginning to learn themselves. Until Outsiders learn there can be only one community that comprises all of humanity, wars, violence, greed, and discord of all kinds will continue. Even though small communities may have great survival solutions, they will be useless if they keep them just for themselves."

Calile, who had stopped for some of Jom's wonderful stew simmering on his potbellied stove, spoke up. "Well, isn't that what we are doing now, right here in Dream?"

"That's true," Gara answered. "But until *all* Dreamians know themselves to be one community, they won't be of any use to Outsiders. At this point, there are a few who don't think this way in Dream. Nearly everyone else has learned a great deal from Philia's meetings. Dream is becoming more and more unified."

Cavin, who was sweeping the floor, spoke up. "Gara," he said, "almost everyone comes to this store for something. When I was small, people would come here intent only on what they wanted. They would hardly acknowledge each other, and they'd be very demanding.

"Now there's a new awareness. It's as if each person who enters feels what is affecting everyone else, their joy or sorrow, their peace or pain. This happens because their eyes, both inner and outer, are open to whatever they encounter. They are becoming like children, who instinctively know no other way. Adults know that vulnerability is a risk, but they are willing to take that risk because they know it is the only way to *really* communicate with each other.

"Just in this store, while I've been growing up, I've seen the people who come in here being more friendly and open with each other. They used to hardly speak, but now they communicate and seem to care about each other's hopes and fears. A true community is coming about."

Gara smiled and bobbed her head in assent, "That's true, Cavin," she agreed. "We can't have long to wait for the Eclady of each person. That will complete the preparations for our mission. If any stragglers remain, they will have to be left out, if they choose, or be brought into the fold. The Rock of Knowing must be found, too."

Gwileth, who had just arrived, said, "We have evidence that the Rock of Knowing is in the Craggish hills and that Golo knows where it is. Perhaps we can form a group and get Golo to lead us to it."

Everyone gasped. "But Golo wants to destroy this town and all of us," said Cavin.

Gwileth smiled. "Golo has had a change of heart and has become our ally. He will cooperate in any way he can."

"This is good, but surprising, news, Gwileth. Are you sure it's true?" asked Gara.

"It's a fact, and everyone will know all about it soon. So please, decide who will go. I'd like to be part of the search party," said Gwileth.

By this time many people had gathered in the little store and it had become crowded. A loud buzzing filled the store as the excitement mounted. "It has begun," Gara said to herself, and, slipping out of the store, walked home to the Wise Women in the schoolhouse.

Chapter Thirty-Eight

*L*ife on the farm had completely changed since Gerran had been able to get around again. Darsa and the children were enjoying each other's company and sharing their ideas so well in everything they did that it was a joy for them to be there together. They allowed Gerran to be with them when he chose, but ignored his negativity until he gradually found that joining in their good cheer was much pleasanter for him than his old habits.

When Gwileth returned home with soap and honey, Darsa met her as she climbed the porch steps, and helped her carry her barterings into the kitchen.

"While you were gone, your father decided to go into the orchards with Larso," Darsa said excitedly. "Oh, Gwileth, it's so marvelous. They're beginning to enjoy each other. They went off discussing what had to be done to the trees to keep them bearing, and I noticed that for a moment your father forgot to limp. When they came back—it was even more remarkable—I heard Gerran tell Larso what a good job both of you had done while he was sick."

Gwileth felt her mother's elation and joined it with her own. "I'm so glad, Mother," she said. "Just a short time ago we wouldn't have thought this could happen. It's hard to believe even now."

The men were in the living room drinking palla wine, still talking about the orchard, when Gwileth joined them.

Gerran looked up and said, "You and Larso did well with the trees. They have the appearance of being cared for. They're growing well. Thank you."

Gwileth felt Gerran was *seeing* her for the first time in many years. When he had been particularly disagreeable to her in the past, she had tried to remember those times when he'd taken her to swing among the sweet-scented palla blossoms. Then, whatever room they were in that felt dark, seemed to get lighter.

For his part, Gerran flashed back to the time when he had been twelve and rescued his little sister, Sril, from where she hung on a tree branch. He remembered the way she had looked at him, the way his heart had opened. Am I again feeling such feelings? he wondered now. I've been so afraid for so long that no one would pay attention to me if I showed my soft side. I've closed myself off from everyone.

Gerran saw his family for the first time, as if through new eyes. I've missed a lot, he thought. It may be hard to make up for lost time, but I'll try. I wonder if this is the Eclady I've been hearing them talk about.

They were nearly finished lunch when there was a knock on the door, and before anyone could rise Golo entered. When Golo saw Gerran, he turned and started to go out again, but Darsa called to him. "Come in, Golo. We're glad to see you."

Golo's appearance had changed so much since their last encounter that it was difficult for them to recognize him. He was neatly dressed. The greatest change was in how he held himself. His self-confident, friendly look contrasted with the disheveled appearance and angry face he had greeted everyone with in the past. His light was bright, too.

"I've come to invite you to a meeting in the mound," Golo said.

"I was wondering what that was," said Larso.

Gwileth echoed him, "It's been there quite a while, hasn't it?"

Golo looked at the two young people and thought: How wonderful they are. Gwileth's look is so direct and pure. Larso's inner beauty shines in him. They must be able to see anything.

"For you it has," he replied, "but I only saw it for the first time a couple of days ago."

"Brul and Sheil told us about it at the last meeting," Larso said. "What's going to happen there?"

"It will be a special meeting for all Dreamians," Golo said. "Do you remember Byphon the cladloc?"

"Of course," Gerran said. "He helped to save quite a few people, and it was wonderful when he pulled our placyl into the air. He seemed to be very wise and kind, too."

"Well, he was the builder of the mound. He will be with us at the meeting. He says it's important that everyone be there."

"Will you come?" Golo asked Gerran. "I remember how kind you were, and how distraught I was after the plague when Byphon took you to other bereaved Dreamians. Please come. Maybe Darsa, or one of your children, could bring you in your placyl. Or I will gladly get you. I'll show you the improvements I made on mine."

All looked at Gerran, expecting him to refuse, but he said, "Golo, I'd love to see what you've done to your placyl. I'm sure there will be changes we'll want on ours."

Gwileth got a plate for Golo and offered him some food. He looked at each of them, then said, "Thank you for letting me deliver my message and your kind offer of food. I'd like to stay, but I have to get back to my boys. We have plans for this evening." He shook his head. "I'm still amazed at what wonderful young men they have become, in spite of the kind of father I've been to them."

"We need to find the Rock of Knowing, Golo," Gwileth said.

"Yes, Gwileth, I know, but something very strange has happened. I've lost all memory of where I found it. It's as if all memory of it was erased from my brain."

"We have to find it, so it will be found," said Darsa.

Chapter Thirty-Nine

When Gara got back to the schoolhouse, she found her fellow crones in a state of excitement.

"I've brought you all the things you asked for, and good news," she announced as she came through the door. Fado, not hearing a word, said, "Gara, you're back just in time to hear what we have from Jad in New York."

It was obvious no one was going to listen to her until they finished their communications with the Outside, so Gara joined hands with Laif and Mytil. Immediately, she heard Jad's voice clearly. To make herself more comfortable, she let go of Mytil's hand for a moment. This cut the current that connected all of them, and she got glares from everyone. Gara quickly rejoined hands and settled in to listen.

Caal was asking Jad about the people he saw and contacted every day and about those in other parts of the world about whom he read. "What do they have in common?" she asked.

There was a long silence. "Do you think we've lost him?" Fado wondered aloud.

Jad's voice resumed and it sounded as if it were coming from a chasm. "I have given much thought to this, and I've done some research. Every person I have found out about, no matter what color or culture, is the same as every Hortishan, as I remember them. Each is a physical, emotional, mental, and spiritual being. The millions that inhabit Earth, unless they are impaired, have these characteristics. Yet no two are alike. This diversity fascinates me, and has done so ever since I found myself here."

Jad's words became slower and harder to hear. "He's going into that unreachable state where he's no longer in touch with his thoughts, but if we wait a while he may come back," said Mytil.

Often when they had quizzed him, Jad was sleeping on the sidewalk of one of New York's busy streets. He had found and curled up in some blankets over a grate where warm air arose. In other interrogations, Jad had told the Wise Women how he got there. He'd awakened in a men's shelter, instead of being frozen to death in the mountains as his family in Dream had thought. He told them what a shocking experience it had been.

Early on, when someone had seen his light, he had to fabricate a tale to account for it. From then on he kept it well hidden. He said living on the streets had been an education for him. A passion to understand people had developed in him until he no longer had other interests. Jad found, after living in the city for several years, that to have a law degree was an asset, so he worked hard to get one from a college. He saw that the power one could have by practicing law could be used for evil or good. To his dismay, he found few of his fellow lawyers weren't greedy; few were not blind to the true needs of the people they served.

The Wise Women implanted in Jad's mind the idea that the people of Hortishland would join him someday to bring help to Outsiders. As their suggestions sank into his mind, they became his mission.

By working hard and using his astute mind, Jad had made enough money to live wherever he wished, but he chose to stay on the streets. He enjoyed the friendship; he liked serving the needs of those he knew and liked best. They were simple people with none of the pretenses of the privileged whom he met through his work.

Many of his street companions, though they had incapacitating problems, were intelligent, caring people, generous with their meager possessions. Their greatest problem was a lack of self-worth. He knew that if he could somehow instill into their lives some of the wisdom of the Laws of the Prophecy (he was absorbing these unconsciously in his sleep), their lives would have meaning. They would know they were not helpless and homeless, and that by taking responsibility for their lives, they could find hope where once they had only despair.

As part of his work to learn all he could about people, Jad found a job as a journalist for a big newspaper. He had become acclaimed, and while keeping his Dreamian identity hidden, had a life that few of his Dreamian peers could imagine.

When Laif had asked him what "money" was, Jad patiently explained that instead of bartering, people on the Outside used pieces of paper and coins. This was their "money," and they used it to make their transactions. They also had cards that took the place of money, and big buildings called "banks" where it was managed.

For many Outsiders, money was more valuable than the health and welfare of their fellow humans, Jad said. They worshiped it; some stole it from others, not just by taking it, but by cheating and confusing those who trusted them, living their lives at the expense of those they wronged. There were healers like Drinney, here and there on the Outside, but since everything for Outsiders cost money—food and clothing, every service—the people who had to get help for their illness had to give money to those who attended them. Many had hardly enough for food and shelter, let alone health care.

The greatest problem with Outsiders was their endless vying to have more, to look better, to stand out in any way they could, and to put others down in the process. The worst part was they didn't think about what they were doing. As Jad saw it, they lived by rote, hardly reflecting on their actions. Most walked about like automatons, living each day mindlessly.

"Some of my friends have no possessions at all," he told the Wise Women. "Yet they seem to be as happy as those who have a great deal. I'm trying to find out why."

There was a wonderful building, fifty times larger than the farmhouse in Dream, called a library. It had beasts called lions made of stone in front of it. Inside were shelves full of books, millions of books. Here he spent most of his time reading.

Meanwhile, Jad was oblivious that anyone was listening to or manipulating his thoughts. He was unaware of anything other than living his life, following his desires. He hadn't any idea the Wise Women had filled his dreams with the work that Philia had guided and overseen in Dream since he had left. He was learning by osmosis what Dreamians were learning at their meetings. He stirred in his sleep, making a sound the Wise Women had heard from other listenings. It buzzed in Caal's head. Mytil, Gara, Fado, and Laif heard it too, and were delighted. Jad was snoring. "Maybe we can bring him back now if we concentrate," said Caal.

They said together, "Jad, we need your thoughts. We lost you. Please come back."

Almost instantly they heard Jad's voice again. It sounded as if it came from deep within the Earth. "There is starvation here," he said, "but the worst is not hunger for food or things. The real starvation is for the spirit. Too many lives are empty; wars abound; and only a very few Outsiders trust each other, or themselves.

"It is rare for them, unless they are lovers, to look deeply into one another's eyes, or to talk about subjects that are serious or involve personal thoughts and feelings. Even then they may hide their truths. People can be close, even intimate, for long periods, but never really learn what is beneath the other's surface. There are many experts on what to do and how to do it, but few are aware of the oneness of people. So nobody knows that what they do to others they do to themselves.

"Most parents love their children when they are very young. But they lack the knowledge of how to keep that love flowing over the years. They often lose their connections, and when the children become adults, children and parents find they hardly know each other. They yearn for the love that they haven't learned how to give or receive. It's an unhappy circle."

Jad was silent, finished with what he had to transmit.

Fado said, "Thank you, Jad," even though she knew that he didn't know she was communicating with him.

"Isn't it exciting," she said to the others. "We're gradually getting enough information to help all Dreamians to be well-informed about the Outsiders. Philia will be pleased at our progress. We can report on it at the meeting in the mound."

"Ah yes, the mound," said Laif. "Well I, for one, am eager to see what's inside that strange-looking lump."

"We all are. Now—are you ready to hear *my* news?" Caal could wait no longer. "Listen to this," she announced, before anyone could stop her. "Gwileth told us at Jom's store that Golo has somehow completely changed and wants to help in any way he can. Many were skeptical, but Gwileth assured everyone that it was true. Not only that, she says he's seen the Rock of Knowing. She wants to go with him to it. Don't you think it would be good for us to go, too?"

The women nodded in agreement. "Gwileth told us Golo had *found* it," Caal said firmly. "But since he wasn't at our meetings, he didn't know *what* he had discovered. Now he can't remember where he found it, so it may not be easy to retrace his steps. Yet we'll see what we can do."

Chapter Forty

*G*wileth awoke to feelings she had never had before. She felt an inner excitement catapult her out of bed, and her heart was pounding, as if she'd been running hard. She heard voices in the house, and the air itself seemed to smell different. She dressed hurriedly and went down to find out what was going on. At the bottom of the stairs Larso was waiting for her, his eyes flashing.

"Gwil," he said. "Drinney, the Wise Women, Golo, and Brul are waiting on the porch. They say the time has come to find the Rock of Knowing. They want to start right away. Sheil and Nila stayed home with their new daughter, and couldn't come. Golo says they were secretly given to each other a year ago, before they were reconciled as a family."

"I know," said Gwileth. "I joined Drinney in helping with their giving. We got as many of their friends together as we could. It was wonderful. So much was happening, with the mound, with Golo changing such a lot. We thought it wise to keep it quiet. Casa was thrilled to have a new son, and now that Golo has joined us again he is delighted with his 'new' daughter. The thing is, when I woke up, I *knew* something was about to happen."

She saw Darsa in the kitchen and asked, "Are you going to come with us?"

Darsa smiled and said, "No, I'm going to stay home with your father. It's such a beautiful day. We'll take a picnic to the palla orchard, and talk about when we first met, where life has brought us. We have a lot to talk about. I've put some food together for you, so you can go right off and not hold up the searchers." Then she paused, and added, "I had a dream last night that the Rock of Knowing was on our table and we were sharing pieces of it with every Dreamian. You'll find it."

"Thanks, Mother," Gwileth said, and looking into her mother's eyes, she knew they had become like two individual songs that now made harmonious music together.

Gwileth hurried onto the porch and found Golo apologizing.

"I'm afraid I won't be much help to you. I have no idea of where to look," he confessed. "I do know where I started, and I'll take you there, if you'd like. I'm sure I'll know the Rock if we get near to it. It has power. But you'll know it, too."

"Don't worry, Golo," Larso assured him. "If we're meant to find it we will, and I have a feeling that we are meant to. Let's get going."

The group started toward the schoolhouse, and, as they proceeded, everyone they met joined them until they became a crowd moving on an important mission. Golo led them to the woods that came down the Craggish hills almost to the door of the barn.

"This is where I started," he said. "But there are no paths through the woods, and it's very easy to get lost. I'm not sure how I managed to get home."

"Well," Drinney said. "It looks as if we had better figure some way to keep in touch as we look. How about whistles? I have a lot of them in my classroom. Some people will have to stay close together and share a whistle in case there aren't enough." Drinney rushed off and was back almost before she was missed.

"Here they are," she said as she handed the whistles out. "When the sun is making long shadows and the leaves shimmer in the light, start back whether or not you have found anything. We don't want anyone to get lost. You all know how dangerous that is."

Gwileth and Larso started out together. Neither of them had been in such thick woods before. It was cool and damp, and the woods smelled of leaves and moss and every tree lent its scent to the air. Brother and sister inhaled the aromas, and felt filled with joy. How beautiful! they each thought, in their own way.

Gwileth saw a small clearing where rings of mushrooms sprouted up in profusion. She had heard that Outsiders called them "fairy rings." She went to look at them and to sample them. She picked a few to offer Larso, but he had disappeared. This keeps happening, she thought. It doesn't make sense to blow my whistle, so I'll search on my own.

There was a big mushroom ring on the side of the hill, and Gwileth had a strong desire to sit in the middle of it. She felt as if she were sleepwalking and had no command of her actions. The ring drew her like a magnet. It was where she had always wanted to be.

She sat still and straight. Music surrounded her. She felt as if she were among her ferns again and started to meditate. She heard music coming from within her, so exquisite was its beauty it was both pain and rapture. Then a voice spoke to her from out of the music.

"Gwileth, my child, you are about to begin the life mission you were born for in Hortishland. Now you will prove the mettle that helps you to be what you want to be, to do what you want to do. Can you tell me what that mettle is?"

Gwileth heard herself answering, from that same deep center from which the music flowed. I am speaking with myself, she thought, with the self that I have begun to know deep within me. This is the self I can trust when I am in my truth, where I know everything I need to know. My truth is clear then, even when I don't want it to be, or don't like what it tells me. My mettle gives me the courage not to allow anyone or anything to change what I stand for. It doesn't allow me to do anything just to please others, to be flattered by their approval or threatened by their wrath, or even by death. My mettle saves me from playing the games that others may try to lure me into to betray myself.

Gwileth had forgotten where she was, but still the voice and the music continued. "You have learned your lessons well. Now go and find the Rock of Knowing."

In the woods ahead, Gwileth saw the others, except for Larso and Brul, waiting for her. They had been blowing their whistles, but Gwileth's inner music had prevented her from hearing them. Somehow, the sun had already passed its zenith, but was only beginning to go down. There was a little time left.

"Where have you been?" Drinney asked her. "You look different. Are you all right?

Gwileth was still over-full with the music, and she felt a little giddy. Drinney looked at her and thought: This is no longer a girl. Something has happened. She has become a young and wise woman. The Wise Women, observing Gwileth, thought: Yes, she is one of us.

"I'm all right," Gwileth said. "I don't know why, but I am being pulled toward those magnificent elpalm trees over there."

She started walking toward the trees and the others followed. Just as she got close to them, the trees burst into flame, but they did not burn. The flames leapt from the trees and wreathed Gwileth's head, yet they were not hot to the touch.

Larso and Brul saw the flames around Gwileth. They ran to help her, but seeing her beaming, they stopped in amazement. "What's happening?" Larso asked. Everyone was so astonished that they were speechless.

The young men were carrying something that looked like clay. "Larso thinks it's the same clay that Drinney used to make a cast for his father's leg," said Brul. "Is it, Drinney?"

But before Drinney could answer, Gwileth said, "It is. We'll have to work on it right away. We have just enough time left." She spoke with such authority that everyone was ready to do her bidding. As she spoke, flames surrounded Larso's head, making a corona as on Gwileth's.

"Wow," said Brul. "Look at that, Larso. Your head is on fire, too."

But Larso was intent on the job he was doing. Everyone knew that time was of the essence now. With Larso's guidance, the group molded the clay into a tray, and almost as soon as it assumed the desired shape, it hardened, yet remained light.

"Now it needs a small hole in the center near the edge, and a strong rope of vines to pull it," said Gwileth. "Then we will be ready."

Drinney knew which vines to use and she and the Wise Women made a sturdy rope from them. Larso and Brul threaded it through the hole in the tray. Gwileth started to run, and the others ran after her.

She ran as fast as she could, not knowing where she was going. It felt to her as if she were on a leash, and that she had to run so as not to have it hurt her nor to break it. There was no path, but whatever it was that was pulling her seemed sure of its destination. At first, she tried to pull back and get her bearings, but to no avail. So she gave in and relaxed, and went wherever she was drawn.

"Do you know where you're going?" Larso asked her.

"No idea at all," Gwileth answered, "but I have no choice. I'm being taken to wherever I must go."

As she spoke, in spite of the fact that they were running away from the setting sun, it was becoming light ahead of them.

Gwileth stopped. "There it is." She pointed toward the light. Tears ran down her face. "Our task is accomplished."

"At last," Larso said. His vision was also heightened. "We did it. Our mission is complete."

The rest of the group only saw fog lit from within. Then Gara exclaimed, "I see it! The Rock of Knowing!"

The fog slowly lifted to reveal a rock the size of a very large pumpkin, pale pink with a silvery sheen. "That's it!" Golo shouted, rushing toward it.

"So that's what the clay is for," said Larso, realizing that the power that had guided Gwileth had been passed to him. "Please put the tray here on the ground," he said, as he took charge of the next moves.

As everyone rushed to comply, the Rock started to move. The ground began to shake, and the group held on to each other as the Rock slowly came toward them and settled itself on the tray.

Chapter Forty-One

They emerged from the woods with their great find in tow as the last rays of the sun illumined them. In their elation, they embraced one another, laughing and rejoicing.

Mytil asked Golo, "Where do you think the Rock should be put?"

Golo said, "I'll take it home with me. There is so much I want to learn about it." But as he spoke, the Rock became lighted from within and started to move again on its own. Its tray moved with it, so the group followed it, no longer amazed.

The Rock preceded the Wise Women up to their haven and settled itself in the middle of their magic circle. It was the original stone. It was Trera's. The Laws that Trera had inscribed on it became visible.

They wondered if the message they had been looking forward to reading would appear. Suddenly, it shone from within the Rock: "Love Is All, And All Is One, Remember." Then it darkened and lost its features, showing no signs of being different from any other rock.

The change was so sudden that they knew that they would never have found the Rock if they had not been prepared for it by Philia. The time of Eclady must have arrived, they felt.

"It seems that our day is finished," Laif said, laughing as she looked at the astounded faces around her.

In a haze, they all exchanged their energy, bringing their lights together, then dispersed to their homes. Golo and Brul went to the mound, the Wise Women to their sleeping quarters, and Drinney, Larso, and Gwileth down the road toward their homes.

The threesome walked slowly, in deep thought. Drinney broke the silence, "So this is it," she said. "The time of Eclady. The time when everyone here will begin to know what they need to know to teach Outsiders how to heal their world."

She looked at Gwileth and Larso with love and admiration. Their crowns were still lit, but less brilliantly than before. "When I assisted in your birthings, it was clear to me that you were vital to the Prophecy. Now, what I felt sure of then, has become true. I am happy for you both, and for everyone in Dream."

Gwileth smiled. "Without you, Drinney, nothing would have gotten to where it now is. You have always been true to yourself, to your calling, and to every person in Dream. You have taught us most of what we know, and ministered to our every need. We all love you very much."

Larso said, "Your patience with me helped me learn and grow. I know sometimes I was hard to deal with. Thank you, Drinney. You've been an angel."

Drinney said, "Thanks, both of you. We have an exciting day coming up tomorrow. I can hardly wait to see the inside of that mound. Let's meet here at my gate, early. I hope your parents will come, too."

"They will," Gwileth promised. "They are like kids who

just found out they are best friends. So much has changed. There is joy in our home now, all the time."

They hugged and said good-night, and brother and sister continued toward the farm. The lights in the house greeted them, as did their trogs and a delicious aroma they didn't recognize. Darsa and Gerran sat at the table drinking brin cider. They saw the radiance their children emanated.

"What happened?" Darsa asked. "You must have found the Rock. You seem so elated. We want to hear everything."

Chapter Forty-Two

*D*awn came clear and fresh, and the four Bavreses were up and about early. Gwileth and Larso told their parents all about their fiery wreaths and the excitement of finding the Rock. It was a beautiful beginning for the day.

Gerran was well again and only limped a little at the end of the day if he forgot to take a break from his palla orchard or had been standing too long. He was a pleasure to be around. He enjoyed his wife and children so much that the family was happiest now when they were together.

After breakfast, they headed toward Drinney's. She opened her door, and came out of her house as they arrived. They greeted each other and Drinney told them Fado had come by earlier to tell her that the Rock of Knowing had left Crone's Heaven on its own during the night and had ensconced itself in the mound.

Drinney greeted Gerran as joyously as anyone else, as if his joining the group were nothing special. Her warmth melted any misgivings he had about her, and he thanked her for setting his leg, and for the numberless ways she had helped his family.

Gerran was surprised at himself. I have changed almost as much as Golo, he thought. No one forced me to do anything. It was important for me to discover that force only produces resistance. Loving firmness and justice feel better. They allow anyone to choose their own path. My choice of Darsa for my given was the best decision of my life.

"You are very quiet, Gerran," Darsa said.

"Yes," said Gerran, as he took her arm lovingly in his.

"Have you been to the mound before, Drinney?" Gwileth asked.

"No, but, a few weeks ago Sheil and Nila came to see me, and urged me to come. I'm excited. It must be wonderful." Drinney danced along.

The day was cool and fresh, and Dream's families were streaming out their doorways, swelling the size of the group. The residents of Dream approached the mound. It exhibited a glow that attracted those near it. People were saying to themselves, How long has this been here? Why haven't I noticed it before? Isn't it beautiful?

Ariel stood at the entrance, and each Dreamian felt in awe of his beauty and power before entering. They were greeted by music, the scent of flowers, the aroma of earth, and blissful feelings. In the middle of the space was the Rock of Knowing, ablaze with its own light.

Everyone felt their hearts open.

There was room for all. The light changed and Philia appeared, radiant as usual. This time, there was something different about her that everyone recognized, but couldn't define. Her light was the same as in the past, but they felt it penetrate their hearts in a new way. She was silent for several minutes, looking at the group, her face one of delight and compassion. Then they heard Byphon's voice, as purple and green lights on the ceiling pulsated.

"Welcome," he said. "This is the culmination of Hortish history. You are all here, ready to go Outside and show what you have learned to those yearning for the joy you know to be part of their lives. Philia and I will be with you wherever you are. Call on us at any time."

"Thank you, Byphon," Philia said. "Much has taken place in Dream since my last visit. So much that you are now ready to graduate to your next assignment. As I have reminded you many times, the reason for Hortishlands is for every person to become so aware of the purpose of being human, that it becomes clear there is no other way to live. Every one of you has learned from the Prophecy and the struggles in your lives that nothing else is important. You have become in-lighted. You can see this by the brilliance of your lights. Look at one another. You will see differences in the appearance of every one of you since our meetings began. It has been gradual, so you may not have noticed."

Philia, hovering in the air, smiled at the Dreamians, who were smiling at her. They were amazed to see her words were true. Now they saw she stood on a small platform of light that illuminated everything in the mound, in concert with the bright lights on everyone's head.

The Wise Women checked person to person to see how they were doing. Some were overwhelmed by the beauty of the sights and sounds, and needed to be calmed. Some were awestruck and had to be reassured nothing frightening was about to happen. The Wise Women were bringing everything together.

"Is everybody here?" Philia's voice rang clear and true, like chimes.

"We've checked all the houses of Dream. No one is missing," Jom announced from the back. "All of us are here, even Piren, the daughter birthed to Golo's son, Sheil, and Cassa's daughter, Nila."

Jom's hair had whitened and his features had grown

stronger and more distinguished and were filled with love for everyone. His eyes twinkled with his ever-present humor.

Inside the mound, there was a large raised platform and on it were many small bags. Philia said, "You may each take one of the bags. In every bag there is a small round stone. It can make you invisible for as long as you choose. I recommend that you try it out. You will only be invisible to Outsiders, not to each other. To each other you will look pale, and the light on your head will be green. You will be meeting Outsiders soon. You will know you're invisible by the very small blue light that only you can see on your left wrist. Also by the fact that Outsiders will walk right through you.

"Something you have noticed and surely wondered about is a little flap on the inside of your right wrist. It is where you will keep your small, round stone from now on, where you will put it when you are not using it. You do not have to fear losing it. When you rub your arm with it from side to side, you will become invisible. Can you guess where it came from?"

"The Rock of Knowing," someone shouted.

"That's right," Philia said. "If you had not found the Rock of Knowing, if Golo had not studied and learned its powers, your entrance into the Outside would have been too precarious. You would have run the risk of being killed. Golo has charged every pebble permanently so that its only power is to bring about invisibility. You need not worry about any other effects, although the Rock itself has many other powers, which will be studied and made available in future generations."

Each Dreamian looked at their pebble, surprised to see in tiny letters the words, "Listen, listen, listen, and respond with love."

Several lights began to glow blue on wrists. Someone exclaimed, "But how can we know if our lights on our heads are showing?"

"You will feel a prickling feeling in your neck when it is on, and none when it isn't. Don't be afraid. It will not bother you in any way, and you will get used to it. It will be a great protection until you get to know and understand your fellow humans on the Outside.

"When you rub the stone up and down, you will instantly become visible to whoever is close enough to see you. So be aware and use it wisely. You will also be able to retract your lights, so as not to appear different from Outsiders when you are with them. Remember, you are there to share your learning, to guide and encourage Outsiders, to help them find the purpose they were born for. You will bring about love and harmony wherever they are lacking."

A voice that seemed to come from within each Dreamian announced in triumph, accompanied by trumpets and singing: "There shall be no separation. Christian and Jew, Muslim and Buddhist, all indigenous peoples, Farsis, Hindus, Sikhs, every organized religion—all can find delight in their diversity. Many will lead the way, glorying in the fact that all are one humanity, whatever their color or differences, wherever they are on this planet."

From her shining platform, Philia expanded her mantle of light to encompass each of them. She looked more solemn and imposing than usual. "Our time is pivotal for humanity and the Earth. Through the lessons each of you has learned as you achieved your Eclady, your kindred beings, the Outsiders, will be given a choice. They can destroy the Earth or learn the joy of preserving the planet. Outsiders must learn that they are not separate from the Earth or from each other, and that what they do to one, they do to themselves. They will learn to make connections between everything, and then rise up to see the whole they have created. This is the last time you will see me, but I will always be with you."

They heard Philia's voice, as from a distance, saying, "You have learned well. The Eclady is in place. Each of you has learned who your true Self is and is living from that inner knowledge. Now put your learning to good use. It is sorely needed."

The people of Hortishland realized the boundaries of their world, which they had always thought were permanent, were lifting, like huge screens. A new landscape appeared before them, and Hortishland was no more.

Chapter Forty-Three

J rose from my word processor and heaved a sigh of relief. At last I had done the best I could to record what Larso had revealed to me, mixed with the many images I had had of the world of Dream. I hoped that mitigation of the suffering and confusion in my world, the Outside, would come. This is what had originally spurred me on to discover Hortishland and its people. I had grown to love each one of them, and already was missing them. I hoped we would meet again.

That man who sold me a newspaper yesterday—he had such a twinkle in his eyes. . . . Could he have been . . . Jom?

As I started to close down my computer, there was a knock at the door. I went to see who it was, but before I could get to it, there he was, standing in the middle of the room. Of course I recognized him instantly, in spite of the fact that he was young, clean-shaven, and wore a business suit.

"Larso," I said. "How wonderful! I wasn't sure I'd ever see you again."

He smiled, and it felt to me as if the sun had suddenly come out on a dull and foggy day.

"How do I look?" he asked. Then he asked again, "Do you think anyone who sees me will guess I'm not an Outsider?" He sat down and let the light on his head shine. It was so bright I squinted. "This is great," he announced. "I can relax with you. You know all about everything, so there's nothing to hide."

"Just don't forget that when you're not here," I warned him. "If anyone sees your light, you'll cause a riot." I gave him a cup of tea and a scone with a Hortish coin on top.

"You kept it," he laughed. "Now that I'm in this world where everyone thinks time is so important, I can appreciate how *long* you've saved it. The people I'm meeting here remind me of the people of Dream, of what they were like before the plague. You haven't answered my question. Will people think I'm an Outsider if I appear the way I am now, without my light shining?"

Looking at him, I saw a young man, as handsome as any I had ever seen. But even more importantly, I saw a person of undeniable integrity; it shone through his eyes. I saw his life spread out before me, the little boy hiding under the chair, the mature man in front of me. As I looked deeper, I saw a wonderful old man with a white beard. The man he would become, the same one who visited me even before his birthing in Hortishland, however paradoxical it seemed.

"Yes, yes," I said. "Of course. It's hard for me to remember how time is. Every yesterday is in today, and every today is in every tomorrow. You will do well blending in. People won't know you haven't always been one of them. My world is starving for what you've learned and what you have to offer. My blessing goes with you and all the Hortishans from all over the world who are among us now. They will help those who think they have no choices to know that at any moment they are free to say yes or no, to anything, and that they will be given the courage to do so if they want it."

I pulled myself back from those wonderful eyes, and found that Gwileth had joined us. The light from her head looked like Fourth of July sparklers, only brighter. I felt myself transported to a world where nature could thrive. Colors, scents, flowers, rocks, waters, insects, birds, and every animal, large and small—all spoke from every part of her. A thrill went through me as I greeted her.

"You did it," I said, feeling how inadequate words were. "Now you will be tested, but you will also gain eternal gratitude. We must hope it's not too late."

"The Rock of Knowing has been placed near the obelisk in Washington, D.C. We put it there to assure all people that a new time has begun. All who stand in awareness next to it will be filled with the strength and light that emanate from it," Gwileth said. "It is also there so no one can doubt that something new from an unknown world has come into this world."

While we talked, a feast appeared on the table and I became a guest of my guests at the most delicious of meals.

As we enjoyed the meal, Larso said, "We wanted to reward you, and thank you for bringing us to life by writing about us. We probably will not meet again. Rest assured, though, wherever you find people coming together to learn that there is only one language, one world community of love and compassion, there we will be. Unless we have not already planted seeds for this and moved on ourselves."

Tears ran down my cheeks and a joy I had not known was possible filled me. We embraced.

A second later I looked around and wondered if I had been dreaming. There was no sign of either of them or of the dishes we'd used. And then I saw it: a lovely palla, in a glorious shade of yellow with little blue dots all over it. It was in the center of the table where we had eaten. I looked more closely and saw that it would not spoil. It was made of an imperishable substance.

"Thank you," I said to the air. "Thank you, thank you."

About the Author

Margaret Lloyd, who divides her time between New York City, South Carolina, and Cape Cod, comes from a background of what she calls "prestige, privilege, and prejudice." She is the great-granddaughter of the noted stained glass artist, painter, and author John LaFarge. She is the mother of four, the grandmother of nine, and the great-grandmother of, so far, one. Her long life—eighty-five at the time of this book's publication—prepared her for this remarkable mythopoeic foray into an alternate world that holds a spiritual message for ours.

Hampton Roads Publishing Company

. . . for the evolving human spirit

Hampton Roads Publishing Company
publishes books on a variety of subjects including
metaphysics, health, complementary medicine,
visionary fiction, and other related topics.

For a copy of our latest catalog,
call toll-free, 800-766-8009,
or send your name and address to:

Hampton Roads Publishing Company, Inc.
1125 Stoney Ridge Road
Charlottesville, VA 22902
e-mail: hrpc@hrpub.com
www.hrpub.com